Harris:

The Return of the Gunfighter

SUNDOWNERS
a division of
Treble Heart Books
1284 Overlook Dr.
Sierra Vista, AZ 85635-5512

Republished and Reprinted in the U.S.A.

ISBN: 978-1-932695-64-9

Thank you for choosing a Sundowners Western

Harris:
The Return of the Gunfighter

H. R. Williams

Sundowners
A Division of
Treble Heart Books

Dedication

**TO BIG MAMA
SHE LOVED A GOOD WESTERN**

WESTERN UNION

TO: Charles Wilkie   FROM: Steven Olsen
     Sheriff, Phillips Co.   Sheriff, Van Buren Co.

RE: Alert Alert Alert
     Seth Jones, James Jones, Bud Jones, and Robert
     Reese, aka Snake River Reese, believed enroute to
     Medford (stop) These men have stated intention to
     do harm to yourself, Dick Wessell, Henry Harris,
     and various ex-jury members (stop) All four should
     be considered extremely dangerous (stop) Further
     details will be provided upon acknowledgement
     (stop stop stop)

Dedication

**TO BIG MAMA
SHE LOVED A GOOD WESTERN**

WESTERN UNION

TO: Charles Wilkie   FROM: Steven Olsen
      Sheriff, Phillips Co.   Sheriff, Van Buren Co.

RE: Alert Alert Alert
      Seth Jones, James Jones, Bud Jones, and Robert
      Reese, aka Snake River Reese, believed enroute to
      Medford (stop) These men have stated intention to
      do harm to yourself, Dick Wessell, Henry Harris,
      and various ex-jury members (stop) All four should
      be considered extremely dangerous (stop) Further
      details will be provided upon acknowledgement
      (stop stop stop)

Nemo me impune lacessit
(no one provokes me with impunity)
—Motto of Scotland

Chapter One

Monday

He rode down out of the hill country, a tall, lean man on a gray horse. Anyone watching would first notice the erect posture and his easy seat in the saddle. A closer inspection would reveal worn and faded clothing with a sweat-stained hat tilted forward, it's wide brim shading his eyes. His eyes were his most prominent feature. Large, luminous, and green, they were in constant motion, the eyes of a man who didn't miss much. Like most men living west of the Mississippi, he sported a gun belt with a pistol jutting from its holster. The tip of the barrel peeked out below, showing where the front sight had been filed away.

His name was Harris, first name Henry, though Harris was the name most often used. He'd been in the saddle all day, and now, having left the hills behind, he halted and lifted the brim of his hat to study the flat, cultivated fields, lying close to dense patches of forest and wild expanses of Johnson grass. Not much had changed since his last visit except there seemed to be more cultivation and less forest. The local farmers were growing more ambitious. He took in the peaceful scene and heaved a tired sigh. Suddenly, a covey of quail burst from a nearby thicket. The rider's head snapped to the left, green eyes widening and his hand dropping toward his gun. Harris watched the birds flutter away and again surveyed the landscape, his senses alert to any other sound or movement. There was nothing save the rustle of wind blowing through the Johnson grass and a vee of geese winging high above, heading southward for the winter.

The dirt road stretched out ahead, thinning into the distance. Harris shifted in the saddle and started the gray mare forward. Off to the left, he occasionally caught sight of the great Mississippi, glinting between the trees. Years ago, he had crossed this river, heading toward the western territories, never dreaming what changes those years would bring. And now, as always, the sight of those wide waters brought a sense of calmness to Henry's soul. He wished the wind were blowing from the east, so he could breath in the river's cool moisture and its scent of hidden fish.

In the distance, he made out the outlines of Medford, a small town of around five hundred people, one of whom had just summoned him. Its framework wavered in the heat waves like a desert mirage, and as Harris slowly approached it, the town reached out and met him with its memories. There were people ahead he could never forget, not the least of which was a dark-haired woman and a gruff old sheriff. The woman would be waiting, as always. And the sheriff? Well, yesterday he had sent his deputy to Harris with a message: "Come quickly, I'm going to need you again." And so Henry Harris was coming, but with a reluctant mind. His old friend and mentor was seeking a man, thought Harris, who perhaps no longer existed.

He reached Medford within the hour and rode down Main Street, his horse's hooves stirring up puffs of dust. Weathered, wooden buildings rose up on either side: a barber shop, general store, two boarding houses, and a livery stable, all lit bronze by the sinking sun. Further on, a red brick structure stood in splendid contrast to its neighbors. This was the Medford City Bank, the only bank in town. Narrow side streets ran off to right and left, bordered by simple frame houses. Front Street, heading eastward, ended at the riverbank, where a loading dock and a couple of warehouses awaited the occasional steamer. At the utmost end of Main Street the rider could make out Kate's Place, a combination restaurant, saloon, and hotel. It stood two stories tall and gleamed under a fresh coat of paint. Harris figured Katie was somewhere inside.

He stopped before a wide wooden building, which, in contrast to Kate's Place, lacked any coating, recent or otherwise. However, SHERIFF'S OFFICE: COUNTY JAIL appeared in neat lettering on a shingle across the front. He dismounted, tied the horse to the hitching rail, and walked inside.

It took a moment for his eyes to adjust to the dim interior. Finally he made out a wooden table, four chairs, a potbellied stove, and assorted wanted posters hanging from the walls. On the left, an open doorway led to the jail cells. The back wall held a gun rack, cradling three Winchester rifles and a shotgun. They'd been recently cleaned. Harris could smell the gun oil. Beneath the guns sat Sheriff Charles Wilkie, behind a scarred, oak desk. The familiar scowl was still in place, but Wilkie's blue eyes somehow belied that expression. They were surrounded by crinkly laugh lines and held a glint of mischief. There was something different, though. Today, Wilkie's face bore a harried, worried look.

The sheriff pushed backward, rose, and shook Harris's hand. "Grab one of them chairs," he growled.

Harris brought a hardback chair from against the far wall, while Wilkie regained his seat. The sheriff reached in a desk drawer and pulled out a bottle and two glasses. He poured them each a whiskey. They tossed down the drinks and Wilkie said, "I appreciate your coming down. I was doubtful that you would."

Harris spoke for the first time. "I needed supplies so I thought I'd drop in."

The sheriff frowned. "Didn't Bubba deliver my message?"

Harris tilted his chair back and said, "Yeah, he delivered it. Said you needed some help, but he didn't say what kind. What kind of help, Charlie?"

Wilkie regarded Henry for a moment, his gaze suddenly solemn. "The kind you're good at."

"So you're expecting trouble."

"That's about the size of it," said the sheriff.

"Is Bubba Dawkins a full-time deputy now?"

"My only deputy, full-time or otherwise."

"Well, there you go. You've already got help."

The sheriff refilled their glasses and put the bottle away. He glanced sideways at Henry and said, "Bubba's coming along, but he's green. He needs seasoning."

"He packs a big gun."

"That old Colt Dragoon," chuckled Wilkie. "Yeah, his Pappy gave it to him. He's sentimental about it. I doubt if he can hit anything with it."

"Low rating your deputy won't make me go along," said Harris.

"*You* were once my deputy."

"That was a long time ago."

For the first time, a doubtful look crossed the sheriff's face. He stared at Harris and said, "So you've decided not to help."

The other man gave a small sigh. "Look Charlie, it may have slipped your mind, but I've got a farm to tend to."

"Yeah, but your crops are all laid by. You won't be busy for another month, and you've got a hired hand to look after the livestock."

"Yeah, and you've got a deputy."

"Humph," grunted the sheriff.

"Besides, I've left that life behind."

"What life?" asked Wilkie, the blue eyes wide and innocent.

"You *know* what life."

"Hell Harris, if you're talking about the killing, you never shot anybody who didn't deserve it. Come to think of it, you never shot anybody who wasn't trying to shoot you."

"Maybe that's what bothers me, all the people who were trying to shoot me."

The sheriff gave Harris a solemn look. "I've never known or heard of anybody that was faster and better with a gun."

"Was is the right word," said Harris.

"Hell," said Wilkie with a sudden grin, the big teeth shining. "I noticed that hog leg when you walked in the door. It ain't been without use. I'll bet you practice every day."

Henry watched the wide grin fade before replying. "Maybe, but that has nothing to do with this."

"But you'll listen to what I got to say?"

"Yeah, as long as I'm here," said Harris. He was starting to feel a lot of enveloping pressure from this relentless lawman. Rising, he walked over to a side wall, and stood studying one of the wanted posters.

"Have you heard of that one?" asked the sheriff, tipping his head toward it.

Henry nodded and continued to stare at the poster.

"And?"

"It's Snake River Reese, a gunfighter out of Denver. What about him?"

"He's related to the Jones brothers, uncle or something like that. He could be riding with them."

Harris turned to face the sheriff. "Riding with them? Charlie, if you'll recollect, the Jones boys are in prison."

"*Were* in prison. They got out a few days ago. Now they're free as the wind and about to blow up some trouble."

"So where are they now?" asked Harris.

Wilkie plucked a telegram from the desk top, walked over, and handed it to Harris. Henry noticed that the sheriff wore the familiar faded khaki pants and shirt, plus a Colt .44, supported by a brown gun belt. It was like a uniform with him. "According to Sheriff Olsen, over in Fort Smith, they're on their way to Medford."

"Well, this is their home, Charlie."

"Yep, but a bartender there in Fort Smith heard 'em talking about their homecoming. Bragged about what they were gonna do to me and Dick Wessell when they get here. Your name was also mentioned. The bartender said they were all in a lather. Even talked about killing some of the jurors who convicted them. They finally lit out. The bartender told Olsen, and Olsen went right to the telegraph office. We've telegraphed back and forth since then."

"So what makes you think Reese is with them?"

Wilkie glanced at the poster of Reese and said, "He was in a gunfight in the same town, on the same day. Needless to say, he was the one left standing. He disappeared about the same time as his nephews. Now, he might not be with them, but as they say, 'blood is thicker than water."

"Could be all talk," said Harris.

"Could be, but I wouldn't count on it, especially if the uncle is with them. The Jones brothers know how to hold a grudge, and your name won't be lost on Snake River Reese."

"So that's why you asked me to come down."

"Uh-huh. We need you. And when I say we, I'm not just talking about me and Bubba; I'm speaking for the whole town."

"The brothers don't know about Bubba, do they? They think Dick is still your deputy."

The sheriff returned to his desk and sat down with a sigh. "I reckon they ain't up on current events."

"But they're gonna be looking for me, regardless," said Harris.

Wilkie gave him a sly smile. "Looks that way."

Harris walked over and stared out the open doorway. Wild honeysuckle grew on a fence across the street and he took a deep breath of its musky aroma. After settling on the farm, he'd begun to notice the small pleasures that his senses could provide: certain sights and sounds, and even the touch of a woman's hand or the sweet scent of honeysuckle. Now, as he thought about the pending crisis and the sheriff's plea, he was reminded of another small pleasure, long hidden away. It was the quiet swell of pride that comes with utter competence, with knowing you might be the very best there is at what you do.

"There's something extra in it for you," came the voice from behind him. "I mean besides the deputy's pay. You also get a cash bonus of one thousand dollars."

Harris slowly turned around, his chin uplifted, the face set. Wilkie read his answer there and his thin lips twitched in a smile.

"The ex-jury members made it up," he said. "At least the ten that's still in town. One hundred dollars each. Evidently, they don't think it's 'all talk.'"

"I reckon not," said Harris. "That's a lot of money, Charlie. I imagine it came dear to some of them." He walked back and picked up the telegram. "When did this arrive?"

"Came in yesterday morning, right before I sent Bubba to get you."

"Yeah, he wouldn't stay the night. Said he had to get back."

"Well," said Wilkie. "Bubba likes his job."

"How far is Fort Smith? About a five day ride?"

"That's right, which means they could be here by the weekend."

Harris lay the telegram on Wilkie's desk and slowly nodded his head.

The lawman nodded back and stuck out his hand. "The county will pay for your room at Kate's. I've already got it reserved."

Harris entered Kate's Place and stood looking around the lobby. On the left, an open passageway led into the restaurant where a dozen tables sat covered with white cloths. A set of swinging doors were set in the rear wall. From beyond came the sound of clinking glasses, laughing voices, and a poorly played piano. The sun had barely set but the saloon was already busy. Harris glanced to the right. A flight of stairs led up to the hotel rooms on the second floor. Near the stairs stood a check-in desk, and behind the desk stood Kate, the old smiling, mocking Kate, looking beautiful as ever, standing like some dark promise for the coming night. She placed both hands on rounded hips, and in a quiet voice said, "Well look who decided to join the civilized world."

Harris, a grin on his face, walked over and said, "How are you, Katie?"

"Not too bad," she answered. "Prospering."

"So I see," said Harris, glancing toward the saloon.

"Oh, it'll get even better in an hour or so."

"Dosh Colson still behind the bar?"

"Yeah, I don't know what I'd do without old Dosh. Except for the record keeping, I pretty much let him run the saloon, *and* control the trouble makers."

"Seems fairly peaceful now."

Kate gave him a sly smile. "Not like the old days, huh, when you rode through town?"

"No," Harris said, "not like the old days."

There was a brief silence while Kate held him with her eyes, the eyes luminous and soft, the look tender and caring. She took a small, graceful step toward him and murmured, "Some of those days were pretty good, Henry. I haven't forgotten."

Harris studied this brown-eyed, woman, with the still shapely figure and the long, ebony hair, and said, "Me either."

A salesman with the ubiquitous carpet bag walked up and stood behind Harris, waiting to check in.

Kate turned around, plucked a room key from its hook, and handed it to Harris. "Room Ten," she said. "At the end of the hall and to your right."

As he turned to go, she whispered, "What're your plans for tonight?"

"Probably have a couple of drinks, eat supper, and turn in early."

"If you can hold off until eight o'clock, I'll join you for supper."

Henry grinned and gave her a quick wink. "I'll try and stay awake."

Harris placed the key in his pocket and strode back outside. He led his horse to the livery stable and returned to Kate's with a string tied package under his arm. He opened the door to his room and nodded appreciatively. The room looked clean and smelled fresh. Both windows were open and a night breeze stirred the curtains. Harris walked over and peered down at the street. A dozen hanging lanterns lit the way and a rising breeze has set them swinging, their back and forth movement casting huge, shifting shadows on the wooden store fronts. Across the street, a window slammed shut and a woman behind the panes cupped her hand and blew out a candle. Except for this place, Medford was closing down for the night. He laid his package on the bed, opened it, and withdrew soap, a razor, and a clean shirt.

After using a wash basin to clean up and shave, he returned to the lobby and entered the saloon. He was met with the sound of loud talk and laughter and the smell of spilled beer and cigar smoke. Henry had spent a lot of hours in places like this, many of them happy ones, and parting the swinging doors felt like coming home.

"Harris!" someone bellowed from the bar, and he knew without looking it was Dosh. He gazed down the mahogany bar and saw the beefy bartender at the far end, polishing a glass and beaming. His bald head gleamed in the lamplight. Harris lifted his hand and walked over.

"How the devil are you, Harris," Dosh boomed. "I ain't seen you in ages."

"Doing well, Dosh."

"You going to be around long?"

"Maybe. The sheriff wants me to do something for him."

Dosh Colson looked at him with narrowed eyes. "To my mind, that something is worth more than a deputy's pay and a thousand dollar bonus."

Harris stared hard at the bartender. "You know about all this?"

"Why sure I do. The whole town knows. You think ten men are gonna shell out a hundred dollars each without telling people about it?"

"I haven't talked to anybody but the sheriff and Katie, and she never said a word."

"Oh, she will," said Colson. "You know Miss Kate. She will, but she'll pick the time."

Harris's face relaxed and he said, "Well, am I gonna grow old waiting for a drink?"

Dosh reached under the bar and brought out a dusty bottle. "Don't know why I bother to hide this. Nobody but you and Miss Kate drink scotch." He poured a shot glass full and pushed it across the bar. Harris lifted it and took a sip.

"So, how've you been, Dosh?"

"Pretty fair. Can't complain. Kate pretty much leaves me on my own and I kinda appreciate that."

"I know what you mean," said Harris. "It's nice to be trusted."

They were interrupted by a slim, young man, who stepped up to the bar and ordered a whiskey. He sported a wispy mustache and long, blond hair. A Navy Colt hung low on his left hip, the grip pointing forward. The young man sipped his whiskey and regarded Harris with cold, expressionless eyes. "You're Henry Harris," he stated.

Harris slowly turned and nodded his head.

"I hear you're a mighty fast gun."

"Where'd you hear that?" asked Harris.

"Oh here, there, all over the place. Matter of fact, they say there's no one better."

"Well," said Harris, "here's something *I've* heard. I heard there's always someone better."

"The young man smiled and said, "Pretty good, myself."

Harris gave him a long level look, the green eyes wide and watchful. The young man continued to smile and said, "But, you know, I believe you're that 'someone better' you mentioned."

Dosh and Harris watched him stroll across the floor and out the swinging doors. Dosh said, "Some big mouth must have told him you were in here. He showed good sense. He'll bear watching in a couple of years."

"Yeah," said Henry, "along with a lot of others."

The bartender gave him a thoughtful look. "It's kind of hard, ain't it?"

"What's kind of hard?"

"Why, being Henry Harris, I guess."

"Well, it's easier than it used to be. Like they say, 'Out of sight, out of mind.'"

Dosh laughed and said, "Well, this time your reputation did some good."

"One of the few times," said Harris. He finished his whiskey, left a silver piece on the bar, and walked back to the lobby. The clock behind the counter read seven o'clock. Kate was nowhere in sight, so Harris climbed the stairs and went into his room.

Lying clothed and flat on his back atop the narrow bed, he closed his eyes and tried to relax. His mind went back to the episode at the bar, and a certain recollection hovered at the edge of his consciousness. It wavered and shifted and finally came into focus. He was little more than a boy, younger than the lad at the bar, but already known for his skill with a gun. He'd never been in a gunfight, never even drawn his gun, except in practice or shooting competitions, but this was something he did well from the very beginning. It was his one great talent, bestowed upon him like a gift, and he determined to exploit it to the fullest. Practice was the only way and that's what he did, practiced until his right hand was numb, then raw, and then bleeding at the knuckles. Two and three hours a day, every day, for years. He drifted from job to job and a large part of his pay went for cartridges.

Even now, he sometimes went through the drill, but it was just to maintain the muscle memory. It was no longer an act he had to think about. His mind clicked go and the thing was accomplished.

What Henry was remembering now was a bar in Texarkana, where he came into his own. He was working at the Circle A Ranch, and all the cowboys rode into town on a Saturday night. One of them, a man called Curtis, had harassed him for months and the youth had quietly endured it. Curtis was a huge, tough bully. He enjoyed being one, and here in a Texarkana saloon, he got to act the part just one more time.

They were sitting around a table, playing cards. A waitress brought a round of drinks and Harris lifted his glass. Curtis eyed him and said, "You think you're going to drink with the men?" Harris lifted the glass higher and Curtis said, "You take a sip of that and I'll slap you out of that chair." It was at this point that Harris's life changed and Curtis's life ended. Henry held the glass, for a moment, then dashed the contents across the front of Curtis's shirt. The big man leaped to his feet, his face scarlet with rage, and with a hand hovering over his pistol, yelled, "Get up and draw."

The other two players stood and backed away. One of them, an older man, said, "Why don't you just whip his ass, Curtis? He's only a kid."

"Naw, this has gone way past an ass whipping. Get up," he said to Harris, "and use that smoke-iron of yours. I've heard you out in the woods practicing on rabbits. Now try it on a man."

The boy felt panic for a moment, then reasoned awareness came, like cold, cleansing water, washing through his brain. So this was how it would come about, and how it would always remain. He would shoot Curtis tonight, if for no other reason than to save his own life, but never again would he quietly take an insult. From this moment on, nothing would ever be the same. He pushed back his chair and slowly stood up. The jade colored eyes bored into his opponent. Curtis blinked once and his hand quavered above the gun butt. Then it darted downward. His fingers had barely touched the wooden stock when Harris's bullet struck him in the chest, slamming him backward over his chair. The bully lay on the floor, gave one shuddering breath, and died.

There had, of course, been repercussions. The sheriff arrived and hauled Harris off to a cell. However, after hearing testimony from the other two cowboys, plus several other saloon patrons, the sheriff released him. He told Harris that, within the hour, he expected to see him riding out of town. Harris was glad to comply. On the way back to the ranch, the older of his companions, a white-whiskered, sun-blasted cowpoke, broke what had been a long silence.

"Don't feel too bad, Henry," he said. "Curtis had it coming."

"Yeah," the other cowboy chimed in, "I never liked the son of a bitch anyway."

"I don't feel bad," said Harris. "He didn't give me any choice."

"That's true," said the older man. "Still, I wouldn't want a thing like that on my conscience" Then, glancing at the young man's set face and staring eyes, he lapsed back into silence.

"Well," stated the other cowboy, "I been to a hoochie kootchie show and two county fairs, but I never seen anything like it."

"Like what?" asked his partner.

"Why, like our boy here, that's what. It won't take long for the word to get out."

"I reckon," said the older man, "and that's a pity."

They arrived at the ranch, but Harris didn't stay long. The owner paid him off and fired him. After all, Curtis had been a top hand.

He'd spent the following years drifting from place to place, serving as a deputy in various dusty towns, hiring out as an enforcer to one or another of the big time ranchers, riding shotgun on a stage coach, bounty hunting. Inevitably, his reputation with a gun grew and spread. And Harris continued to practice until his peak was achieved. He could never get any faster or more accurate. He could never get any deadlier. Eleven gunmen had sought him out and all those gunmen were dead. Dead also were some who'd attacked him during the course of his duties. Henry never completely buried them. Once, a newspaper man had the temerity to ask if he remembered the men he had killed. Henry, in a rare blaze of anger, said, "Remember? Of course, I remember. You think I could forget a man I shot down? I remember them all."

Finally, Harris traveled eastward into Medford. He'd passed through the town before, but this time Sheriff Wilkie hired him as a deputy, and this time Henry stuck. For the first time in his life, he became friendly with the citizens. He met Katherine Mulroney and began to put down roots. Medford became his home and nobody was more surprised than Henry. He was even more surprised on the day he found himself a farmer. And now, almost ten years into a new and better life, years of courting obscurity, there came the wrath of the Jones's. And like an old curse, the challenging quest of a gunfighter.

He pulled out his watch as a soft knock sounded on the door. He arose, opened it, and saw Kate Mulroney, standing in the doorway. The top of her head just reached his chin, and she had a way of turning her eyes upward when she looked at him. That look never failed to stir his blood.

"You about ready?" she asked.

"Sure, Katie. I didn't realize it was eight o'clock."

"Well, I wouldn't have let you stand me up."

Harris walked over and picked up his hat. "No chance of that."

Kate frowned, reached up and lifted the hat from his head. "I'll hold onto this and give it a good dusting. You won't need it in the dining room. By the way, you could also use a haircut."

"You going to do that, too?"

"I've done it before," she responded.

Harris followed Kate down the stairs. She set his hat aside and they walked into the restaurant. A table in the corner bore a RESERVED sign. Kate removed it and they took a seat. She ordered chicken and Harris asked for a steak. The food arrived promptly, along with two foamy beers, and they busied themselves with eating, neither speaking for awhile. Finally, over coffee, Kate looked up and said, "Everyone knows why you're here."

Harris smiled as he recalled Dosh's words. He supposed that Katie now felt the time was right. "Yeah, I know," he responded. "What I *don't* know is why everybody thought I'd take Wilkie's offer."

"Kate shrugged and said, "They couldn't imagine anyone would turn down a thousand dollars."

"Plus a deputy's salary."

"Yes, she said, smiling. "That too."

"And what did you imagine, Katie?"

"I figured you'd turn it down. I figured that, by this time, you'd be on your way back home."

"You were figuring right," he said.

"So what swung you the other way?"

"Something the sheriff told me. He said they were also looking for me."

"Ahhh," she breathed.

"Harris leaned forward and said. "It would only be a matter of time before they came up to the farm, and there'd just be me and my hired hand. Just me, really, because Luke would take off after the first shot. Here, there's Wilkie and the townspeople. Wilkie's tough as an old boar hog, and maybe some of the townies will help."

Kate took a sip of coffee, her little finger poised in the air. "What about the deputy?"

"Wilkie thinks he needs more experience." Harris thought for a moment and shook his head. "Personally, I think he's underrating the man."

"And what about me?"

Harris raised his eyebrows and said, "You?"

Kate placed both hands on the table and gave him a steady stare, her brown eyes lit with fire. "When the time comes," she declared, "just give me a gun. I'll kill anyone who tries to hurt you."

He gave her a prideful look and placed his hand over hers. There was no need for words. They both knew she would do it, but both also knew he'd never see her placed in harm's way.

After finishing her coffee, Kate touched his cheek and left to confer with the restaurant staff, especially the cook. The chicken had not met with her approval. Harris returned to his room, unbuckled his gun belt, and tucked the Colt Peacemaker under a pillow. It had been a long day, most of it spent on top of a horse. He stripped off his clothes and fell into bed. Within minutes, he was asleep.

Sometime later, someone tried the door to his room. The door knob wiggled back and forth. When the person saw the door was locked, a key was inserted and turned. The lock opened with a soft click and the door swung back. Harris was sitting up a bed, clad only in a pair of shorts and holding a very large gun. The muzzle was centered on the shadowy figure in the hallway. The intruder froze at the sight and uttered a faint cry.

"Dang it, Katie," barked Harris. "I might have shot you."

The owner of Kate's Place regained her composure and approached the bed. She brought her face close to his, and with an impish smile said, "Surely, there's something else you'd rather do."

Chapter Two

Tuesday

Harris, contrary to habit, slept late the following morning. He finally awoke, but lay perfectly still with his eyes closed. The other senses, however, were scanning the space around him, taking in sounds and smells and even the movement of air. This precaution, long a habit, was a holdover from the old days. One that had, on at least one occasion, saved his life.

He remembered awakening once on a cold morning in Wyoming. He'd lain motionless beside a dead campfire and heard the sound of breathing, caught the odor of sweat and stale grease. Letting his eyelids raise slightly, he recognized an Indian. Two Trails, bent on a blood feud, had been tracking him for days. Earlier, Henry had killed his brother in a senseless side street shootout. The renegade Sioux sat on a log with a rifle across his knees, black eyes fixed on his victim. Harris raised his head and the warrior found himself staring at a face as remorseless as his own. He grunted and swung the rifle around, but it was the action of a dead man. Harris, sleeping on the trail, always kept his pistol at his side.

Now, the only thing his senses detected was the touch of a moist breeze blowing through the open window and the sound of wagon wheels on the street outside. He yawned and opened his eyes and thought about last night. It was just like old times, hell, better than old times. Kate had always been a passionate partner, but this time she'd quickly taken the initiative, moving with driving persistence, urging him onward. After their lovemaking, she had lain in his arms for awhile, not speaking, but with a soft and peaceful smile on her face. They'd drifted off to sleep, and sometime before dawn, she'd arisen and slipped out the door.

They always got along well together, seemed to fit. Of course, they'd known each other for years, but even from the first, they were comfortable together, at ease with mutual silence. Not for the first time, he pictured them living together, sharing a bed every night, but he knew it would probably never happen. They'd always led two separate and totally different lives. Both were independent and had a lot of the loner in them. She was essentially a businesswoman, a town woman, and would never find contentment on a farm. He figured Kate shared this view because she'd never hinted at anything permanent.

He arose, performed his morning toilet, and went downstairs to breakfast. He drank coffee while the cook fixed up pork chops and eggs. Halfway through the meal, Kate appeared and sat down. She wore a bright yellow dress and looked fresh and rested.

"Hi," she said. Her full lips twitched in a smile.

"Good morning. Get a good night's sleep?"

"Yes, thanks to you."

Harris gazed at her for a long moment. "You're the only one, Katie."

"I know," she said. "So are you." She started to say something else, but halted.

"I know, Katie. Different worlds."

"Yes, my love, different worlds."

Harris returned to his breakfast and Kate ordered coffee. They sat in easy silence. Finally, she leaned forward and he caught a scent of lavender. "Have you given this whole thing serious thought?" she asked.

"Don't have to think much. I believe what Wilkie said. They won't give me much choice. This way, I get to pick the place."

"The place with a thousand dollars in it."

"Yeah, plus the other things I mentioned."

"There's three of them, Henry, and from the stories I've heard, that robbery was the least of their crimes. They're probably all killers."

"So am I," he said with a sad smile.

"There's a world of difference between you and them and you know it. Now, the sheriff is tough, like you say, but he's no gunfighter and neither is Bubba. *You're* the only gunfighter. And those three Jones brothers will kill you any way they can."

"There may be four," said Harris.

"Four?"

"Yeah, Wilkie tells me they might be bringing an uncle."

"Well, that's really great. What's the uncle's name?"

Harris smiled at her darkening face and said, "Robert Reese." He waited.

"Robert Reese," she echoed, flinging her arms in the air. "Snake River Reese, the Denver Gunfighter."

"That's what they call him."

"What the devil are you smiling for? This is serious business."

"I know it is, Katie, and that's the way I'm taking it. I'm about to go see Wilkie. Maybe he's heard something new. Supper tonight?"

She sighed and said, "Of course."

Harris watched her walk away from the table and reflected that there was a helluva lot more he wanted to say to Katherine Mulroney. Up until now, he figured there'd always be time.

Harris entered the sheriff's office and found it dismal and dark as usual. Wilkie sat at the table, cleaning a double-barreled shotgun.

"Charlie, why don't you let some sunlight into this place? It's like a tomb in here."

"It's too hot for more sunlight," the sheriff responded. "And don't be talking about tombs and such. It ain't the proper time."

Harris pulled up a chair. "I reckon you've heard something else."

"Just hearsay, just word-of-mouth, but it seems like Reese is with them."

"What makes you think so?"

"Cowboy, goes by the name of Duff, drifted in last night from Fort Smith. Says he was in Shank's Saloon about a week ago when—"

"Where's Shank's Saloon?"

"In Fort Smith, dammit. Now let me finish."

"Go ahead, High Sheriff," said Harris in a soothing tone.

"Well, Duff says he was drinking in the bar, when he

looked over and who should he see but Snake River and three other guys huddled around a table. Reese had a wide-brimmed hat pulled down over his eyes and kept his head lowered, but Duff recognized him anyway. Says he run with him for a short time, out in the Oklahoma Territory, but finally left him and came over into Arkansas."

"Him and Reese have a falling out?"

"That's just what I asked him," said Wilkie. "Old Duff said that, had that been the case, he'd probably be dead now. Says, he just got tired of watching Reese shoot people, and began to worry that Reese might finally get to him."

"He was talking about gunfights."

"Yep, gunfights. And this cowpoke says that Reese was something to see. Said he was in a class all by himself."

Harris leaned back in the chair and said, "I've heard the same thing." He remembered other things he'd heard, and sat silently, trying to get a sense of the gunfighter, picture him in his mind.

"Anyway, the three guys were drinking and talking pretty loud and one of them called another one 'Seth."

"Seth Jones," said Harris. "Oldest of the three."

"Right, and then Seth says that the four of them are gonna take care of business in Medford. Said it would be easy. Duff sidled past the table with his back turned, anxious to get out of there, when he heard Reese tell everybody to keep their voices down or they could count him out."

"So what do we do now?"

Wilkie gave the shotgun a final swipe with an oiled cloth and replaced it in the gun rack. "We try to round up some more deputies," he said.

"You think those ten jurymen might volunteer?"

"I doubt it. They probably figure putting up a thousand dollars is enough participation."

"You have anybody else in mind?"

Wilkie rubbed his face vigorously with both hands. "Maybe," he said. "At least one, anyway. By the way, you might work at a little recruiting yourself. Start earning your pay."

"I'll see what I can do," replied Harris, "but I'm not hopeful."

"Yeah, I know," sighed the sheriff. "All we can count on is spectators."

A rough wagon road, rutted and dusty after a dry summer, leads from Fort Smith, down through Dardanelle, and onward to Little Rock. On this night, a stagecoach, a few hours out of Dardanelle and enroute to the state capitol, swung around a narrow turn and headed up a grade. A lantern on either side of the stagecoach cast a flickering light on the passing trees and occasionally reflected the fiery eyes of some four-legged forest dweller. This night held the coolness of early autumn, and a soft rumble of thunder was heard toward the west. Inside the coach, its passengers were snugly ensconced and half asleep. Had they been more wakeful, they might have noticed a small campfire, burning at the bottom of the hill.

Four men sat around the low burning fire, over which hung a pewter coffee pot. The coffee made a soft burbling sound, in contrast to the utter silence of the surrounding woods. Three of the men appeared to be related. They bore the same auburn-colored hair and slightly hooked noses. Their beards were long and untrimmed. All three wore faded jeans and print shirts, much in need of a cleaning. The fourth man stood out, not because he bore no resemblance to the other three—although he certainly did not—and not because he was fresh shaven and wearing clean clothing. He was set apart by his bearing and an air of constant alertness. The features, underneath a brushed hat brim, were intelligent and well-formed, and included a delicate, thin-lipped mouth. The eyes were exceptional only in their color. They were an ashy gray, made even more pallid when contrasted with his well-tanned face. Reflected in the campfire, they appeared almost colorless, two restless orbs, moving left and right, missing nothing. He sat upright, as an Indian sits, with both legs crossed in front of him.

One of the three brothers scratched his chest, stared at the pale-eyed man, and said, "Robert, why couldn't we have stayed the night in Dardanelle? We got enough money for a hotel. We could have had a hot bath and slept in a soft bed." His voice held the flat twang of eastern Arkansas.

Another, who appeared to be the oldest, spoke through his beard, "James, quit pestering your uncle. If we'd stayed there, we'd be half a day further from Medford. Also, if you'll remember, your uncle is wanted by the law. It's best to steer clear of towns."

The third brother, called Bud, stretched his arms overhead and said, "We didn't steer clear of Fort Smith, Seth."

"That's because Robert had some business there."

"Yeah, Snake River business," James gave a sharp cackle.

The subject of this discussion continued to gaze into the flames. He neither spoke nor moved and appeared to be lost in thought.

James took a sip from his tin cup, sat it on the ground, and said, "Had we stayed in Dardanelle, we'd be drinking whiskey now instead of stale chicory coffee."

At this, the fourth man lifted his head and fixed his nephew in an unblinking stare. Speaking in a low, even voice he said. "And that's another reason we're camping in the woods. I want no more whiskey drinking until this job is done." A discontented murmur arose and the man continued, "I mean it. You'll all need clear heads for the work ahead, because it won't be easy."

"Well hell, Uncle Robert," returned James. "The sheriff is just an old man, and so is Dick Wessell. Matter of fact, that deputy may even be older."

"What if they recruit more deputies?"

"I don't think that's gonna happen," said Seth. "I was born and raised there and I know the good citizens of Medford. They're an honest, God-fearing bunch with a deep fondness for their own skins. Besides," he said with an ingratiating grin, "when they hear you're coming they'll lock the doors, get in bed, and cover up their heads."

Reese gave them a thoughtful look. "You may be partly right about the citizens, but you're underestimating the sheriff and you should know better. We're all familiar with Charlie Wilkie. Did any of you ever hear of him backing down from a fight?" There was no response and Reese continued, "I'll take that as a no. Now, here's another one for you. Did any of you ever hear of him *losing* a fight?" Again he was greeted by silence. The gunfighter reached out and refilled his cup while his handsome face turned hard. "Of course, we haven't touched on the real danger, have we?"

The brothers shook their heads in unison, because the same name had occurred to all three at the same time.

"Yes," Reese murmured, "Henry Harris."

"Well, he used to have a reputation, "said Bud, "but he's been a farmer for years, and I ain't never seen a farmer I couldn't shade."

"Uh huh," said Reese, "and that kind of thinking *might* just get you killed. If you want to grow old, little nephew, stop underestimating people, especially people like Harris."

Seth tossed a branch into the fire and scowled at the rising flames. "All right, we hear what you're saying, but you got to hear something, too. We *want* that fat-assed Wilkie and his deputy. And we especially want Harris, because he joined in of his own accord. And if anybody who served on that jury pops up, we want him too."

Bud, the youngest, said, "I was sixteen years old when they put me away. That ain't a good age to be in such a place." He savagely poked the fire and added in a husky voice, "We've gotta make them pay."

Seth gripped his brother's forearm and said, "They will, Bud. Depend on it." He locked eyes with Reese and said, "You *see* how it is?"

"Yes, I see," answered his uncle, "and you'll have what you want. Just stay aware of what you're up against. And we'll need some sort of plan."

"What did you have in mind?" asked James.

The gunfighter lay back on an elbow and crossed his feet. "We'll work on it when we get closer to Medford. That way, it'll stay fresh in everyone's mind."

"Well," said Seth, "there's a couple of things to consider right now. Things that might be in our favor."

"What's that?" asked James.

"First of all, they don't know we're coming, so we can take 'em by surprise. The other thing is, they'll be split up. The sheriff and his deputy are in Medford, and Harris will be out on that farm of his, wherever that is. We'll take care of our business in town and then we'll pay a visit on Mr. Harris."

"And how will you handle him?" asked Reese.

"Bushwhack him probably," said Seth. "No need in taking chances, especially if he's as dangerous as you say."

"Don't *you* think he's dangerous?"

"Maybe," said the oldest. "He got the drop on us, so I

never saw him in action. They had us all covered from the git go."

"How did he act?" asked the gunfighter.

"Act?"

"Yes, Seth. How did he perform? Was he, say, nervous, excited?"

Seth gave it a minute; he knew his uncle considered the answer important. "No," he said. "I reckon not. He never said much. It was just a job to him, like shucking corn." He looked at the uncle and added, "But hell, Robert. It'll be four against one. It won't take long to put Harris in the ground."

"No," Reese's voice rang out and three faces swung toward him. "Harris belongs to me. You understand? When we meet, it will just be me and him, and there's *not* going be any bushwhacking."

The oldest brother chuckled softly and took a sip of coffee. "So that's why you're coming along. It ain't just family loyalty. You got to see who's best." He chuckled again and said, "I'll never understand a gunfighter."

One of the four mounts, tethered nearby, stomped a hoof and Bud, always responsive to horses, walked over to them. They could hear him talking in a crooning voice.

Snake River Reese turned to Seth and said, "Well I'm here, and that's all that matters."

"Yep," said Seth, "and you know I appreciate it."

"By the way," said Reese. "I wouldn't stake my life on surprising them."

A quick glance from Seth. "Why not? How could they know?"

"They could *know* because all of you drink too much and talk too much."

"But hell, Robert. That was in Fort Smith."

"There's a telegraph wire running from Fort Smith to Medford," said Reese.

"Well, I don't think anybody heard us."

"Maybe not," said the uncle. "Let's hope not."

A soft snore sounded from across the campfire. James lay flat on his back with his feet next to the flames, his arms flung wide. He blew out a breath and snored again.

"He's got the right idea," said Reese. "Let's turn in. We've got a long ride tomorrow."

Bud returned to the campfire and found all three men asleep. He kicked off his boots, drew a horse blanket over his shoulders, and sat for a long time, looking up at the stars. His thoughts were all about Medford.

Bubba liked being a deputy. He figured it was the best job he'd ever had, far better than working for his Pappy or plowing cotton, where the only thing he had to look forward to was the rear end of a mule. Also, better than working at the livery stable or tending a bar. Of course, the bartending was what led to his becoming a deputy.

He was working at a joint in LaRoche, a tiny hamlet just south of Medford, when he first met Charles Wilkie. The sheriff came into the Butterfly Saloon looking for an armed robber named Donald Lacey, who had, of all things, held up Medford's only dress shop. Sammie Davis, owner of Sammie's Boutique, had identified Donald and wanted his scalp. Wilkie was bound to deliver it to the county jail, along with the rest of the body. He'd questioned a few people and gained zero information. He was about to leave the Butterfly when, lo and behold, Donald Lacey walked in the rear door and up to the bar. Seems he'd been out using the back yard privy. Lacey caught sight of Wilkie in the mirror back of the bar, whirled and drew his pistol just before the sheriff saw him. They stood facing each other and Donald had the drop. Wilkie carefully kept his hand away from his holstered gun and took a few steps toward Lacey.

In a tone of voice similar to the one he would use if he were discussing the weather, Wilkie said, "Well Donald, from the looks of things, I figure you've guessed why I'm here."

"I ain't guessed nothing and I ain't *done* nothing," the robber replied.

"Then why are you pointing that gun at me?" Wilkie took another step forward. "You *are* pointing it at me, ain't you?"

Lacey's voice quavered when he spoke and his gun hand trembled. The sheriff had disconcerted him, standing there so unperturbed. Lacy half expected to see him yawn. "Somebody said you was looking for me. Said you thought I'd done a robbery. Well, I ain't been near no bank."

Wilkie chuckled softly and said, "Oh no, you got it all wrong, Donnie. I don't think you did it. I *know* you did it, and I got witnesses to prove it. Also, as you know, it wasn't a bank you robbed." Here, the sheriff turned in a slow half circle, grinning at the customers, and said, "It was a *dress shop*."

The saloon echoed with laughter and Wilkie added, "Yep, Sammie's Boutique, and I got to tell you, Donald, that surely took some nerve. Old Sammie must be in her sixties, but she's deadly with a brassiere. I hear she uses it like a sling shot." The laughter grew louder and Lacey's face went brick red.

"It's all a damn lie," he yelled and shook the pistol at Wilkie. He looked down at it and cocked the hammer back.

Bubba, standing just behind the culprit, eyed the sheriff with nothing less than awe. He couldn't believe it. Not only was Wilkie ignoring the gun in Donald's hand, he was contemptuous of it, *and* the man holding it. Not content to completely dismiss Lacey as a threat, he was actually goading the man, daring him to pull the trigger.

But whether or not Donald would have shot the sheriff would never be known, because it was then that Bubba pulled a sawed-off shotgun from underneath the bar, leaned over, and placed both barrels to the side of Lacey's head. And for one of the few times in his life, he was completely in charge of a situation and he handled it exactly right.

In an even voice, he said, "Don't even bat your eyes, Donald, or I'll splatter your brains." Lacey remained rigid and Bubba said, "Now, take your finger from around that trigger and turn loose the gun." Lacey didn't hesitate, and as the gun bounced once on the floor, Bubba nodded at Charles Wilkie and said, "He's all yours, sheriff."

Wilkie tied Lacey's hands, and just before issuing him out the door, leaned over to Bubba and said, "Next time you're in Medford, drop by and see me."

And so it came to pass that about a week later Bubba was seated in the sheriff's office and facing him across a desk.

"You know Dick Wessell?" asked Wilkie in his gruff way.

"Yessir, he's your deputy."

"Dick's a good man, but he could use some part-time help." The sheriff looked out from under shaggy brows and added, "We both could."

"Are you offering me the job?" asked Bubba.

"No, not yet." After a pause, Wilkie asked, "What about your position at the Butterfly?"

"It ain't really a position. I'm just filling in for the regular bartender while he's sick."

"Okay, when that bartender gets back, come and see me. The job pays a dollar a day, plus five percent of the fines. You'll be working Friday morning through Sunday night. If you're still interested, I'll give you a try."

A week later, Bubba Dawkins showed up again and the sheriff swore him in. At the beginning, his advice was short and sweet. "Always be pleasant," he said, "and head off violence where you can. But," and here the sheriff slowly measured every word, "you must never, ever, back down from a fight. You must never back away, because if you do, the Sheriff's Office backs away with you. All the Law backs away. Do you understand?"

Bubba assured him that he did, but he couldn't help smiling about the first part. If Sheriff Wilkie had ever displayed a lot of pleasantness, the whole town would be talking, and the word of such a miracle had never reached the ears of Bubba Dawkins.

Bubba had worked his part-time hours for a month and then Wilkie, with the city council's permission, brought him on full time. A few days later, Bubba learned the reason. Dick Wessell, deputy under Charles Wilkie for over nine years, was leaving for Nevada in the fall. He wanted to try his luck, he said, before all the silver ran out.

During Wessell's last months, both he and the sheriff spent a lot of their time tutoring Bubba. Dick never laughed at Bubba's huge gun, and informed him, to the young man's surprise, that a gun, big or small, wasn't really very important. "Of course, you need one or you'd be helpless," he said, "but you'll find that in most situations you'll never have to touch it. The badge will be enough." Then, in the same tone the sheriff had used when he talked about backing away, Wessell said, "Just remember, if you *do* have to pull that gun, you must be prepared to use it. You've got to be geared to kill. And if the killing time comes, you must not hesitate, not even for a second."

Bubba had nodded and taken the advice to heart. He took everything to heart that Dick and Charlie told him and he tried to remember it all. Now, as he headed toward the sheriff's office, he figured his luck, after a lot of grim years, had finally begun to change.

Upon entering Wilkie's office, the deputy saw the back of another man sitting motionless and erect across from Charlie's desk. Bubba watched the man, slowly turning toward him, and then he saw that it was Harris. He walked over and shook the outstretched hand.

Wilkie, in his no nonsense way, said, "Bubba, I need you for a witness. I'm swearing in Harris as my full time deputy." With that, he stood up, administered the oath, and handed Harris a badge.

As Harris pinned it on, Bubba turned to his boss and said, "I figured that was your intention. So where does that leave me?"

"Leave you," barked Wilkie. "Where the hell do you think it leaves you? It *leaves* you in the same place you've been for the last nine months. You're still my deputy. My *chief* deputy, if that makes you feel any better."

Bubba gave a sheepish grin. "I'm glad to hear it, Charlie, but I wouldn't have blamed you. Any sheriff would exchange me for Harris."

Harris listened and thought once more that Wilkie was underestimating this man.

Charlie's face softened and he said, "Drag up a chair, Bubba. We've got some talking to do."

Miles from Medford, a lone man sat underneath an elm tree and contemplated the cook fire before him. The flames licked around a small pot of beans, the man's midday meal. The bean juice bubbled and wood smoke drifted upward through the tree limbs. He removed the container from the fire and sauntered over to his horse, the thin arms and legs moving as if on rusty hinges. Taking a wooden spoon from one of the saddle bags, he strolled back to the pot, dipped the spoon in, and blew on it before placing the contents in his mouth. Slowly and deliberately, he chewed on the beans, and sat cross-legged before the fire.

All edges and angles, he appeared to be nothing but gristle and bone. The pallid, narrow face seemed a stranger to the sun. High, etched cheekbones rose beneath dark, expressionless eyes, and his hair, black as a raven's wing, hung down to his shoulders. The man rose, and in his unhurried way, washed out the pot and spoon in a nearby creek. He ambled back to his horse and tightened the cinch. Taking his gun belt from the pommel, the stranger strapped it around his gaunt waist and drew it to the last notch. The gun belt held a Smith's revolver, its wooden handle roughened by filing. Swinging into the saddle, the man sat for a moment, looking about him at the surrounding trees, early autumn causing the leaves to gain some color. His thoughts turned briefly to the town he was heading toward and the person he was going to see. The thin lips twitched in a smile. Yep, he thought, exciting events ahead. He'd probably take a hand and he was starting to look forward to it. He was glad the wait would be short. Again, there came that ghost of smile, but the eyes did not reflect it. They had seen too much devastation, too many deaths, and they did not light up easily. The stranger nudged the horse with his heels and continued through the woods toward Medford.

"Harris is temporary," said the sheriff. "He probably won't be here more than a few days. We just need him until the trouble is over."

"Yeah," said Bubba. "My landlady is wondering when they'll get here."

Wilkie erupted. "Does the whole damn world know about the Jones brothers?"

Harris shifted in his chair. "Not the whole world, Charlie, but the whole town does. Everybody I've talked to mentions it. Seems your jurors have spread the word."

"Well," said Wilkie, " I had to tell 'em 'cause they've been threatened too."

Harris said, "Did you tell them about Reese?"

"Oh yeah," grinned Charlie, "That's when they put up your bonus."

"You know," said Bubba, "I was just thinking. Since we're all in this together, shouldn't we split that thousand dollars three ways?"

Sheriff Wilkie chortled when he saw the expression on Harris's face. "Don't worry, Harris. Bubba's just joking, or at least I think he is."

"Yeah, I am," said Dawkins, laughing along with Wilkie.

"We're just working dogs, doing our jobs," said Wilkie, "but ole Harris is outside talent, recruited by ten good men, who paid top dollar to get him."

Henry gave them both a rueful smile. "Well, if they shoot me, you two can divvy up the thousand."

"Then I can get that new pistol," quipped Bubba. "I saw it in a catalogue."

"Just don't go ordering it yet," said Harris. "And by the way, sheriff, I thought you said you had a fourth man in mind."

"Yeah, I did," replied Wilkie. "Actually, I was thinking of two men."

"So?"

Well, I been hinting around to Dosh Colson. Even went by his house this morning. He finally got the drift and told me real firmly to forget it."

Harris said, "Now that I remember, Dosh was pretty handy with a gun. Used to be a lawman over in Wichita."

"Well, that's all in the past, according to Dosh. All he wants to do now is tend bar, service that plump wife of his, and eventually die in bed."

"Can't blame him," said Harris. "Anyway, I'd hate to see Kate lose a bartender. What about this other recruit?"

"He may be coming. We'll have to wait and see."

"So what's his name?"

"I just don't want to say right now. Maybe I'm afraid I'll jinx it.

"Sounds like real good help," said Harris. "Well all right, Charlie. Have it your way."

"Now," said the sheriff, "let's talk about our visitors." His gaze focused on Harris. "Do you think they'll come in together?"

"Hard to say. If they don't think the town's expecting them, they may ride in together or they may decide to drift in one at a time. One at a time would be smart; stay separate and stay out of sight until time to make their move. One other thing; their threats about the jurors are probably just hot air. There's no way they'll attempt to murder ten men, or as far as they know, twelve men. They may gun one or two if they're conveniently located, but it's us they want and us they'll be after."

"I think you're right," said Wilkie, "but they don't know we're all together. They'll figure you're at your farm."

Bubba cleared his throat and said, "That could be a problem couldn't it? I mean, how do we know which place they'll go to first?"

"They'll come to Medford first," answered Harris.

Dawkins gave him an inquisitive look. "What makes you so sure?"

"Number one, they don't know where the farm is, so they'll come here to find out. Number two, if they *did* know where the farm is, Medford lays square in their path. They ain't gonna go around the town and then make a two day ride, just to get back to it. Anyway, they'll want to take care of the sheriff first."

Wilkie sighed, placed his boots on the desk. "Sounds reasonable to me. Now, here's my thinking. When the brothers come in there ain't much we can do to begin with. I mean they ain't wanted or anything. All we can do is keep an eye on 'em. Now the sight of Harris will make them draw back a little, postpone things for a bit, and that's what we want, but I figure it won't take long for them to make their play. They may do it as soon as they hit town. The main thing for us to do is stick together. That way, the odds will stay more or less even. Remember, they'd love to get us on a three against one stand. He shook his head and added, "I just hope no citizens get in the way."

"You really think they'd gun us with no call?" asked Bubba. "I mean that's murder of a sheriff and deputies. The federal marshals would take after them."

"I'm sure they know that," said Charlie, "and I'm just as sure they ain't riding all the way from Fort Smith to attack us with harsh language. They mean to kill us. Now, if they can arrange it so it don't look like murder, they're smart enough to do it, especially the oldest one, old Seth. But yes, if it comes down to it, they'll gun us without a call and worry about the marshals later."

"So all we can do is watch 'em?" asked Dawkins.

"Yep, up until they break a law." The sheriff paused and looked at Harris. "Of course, we could maybe provoke them a little. In their frame of mind, that wouldn't be hard to do. And they just might do something that's illegal. Then we can jug 'em all or one at a time."

"Like you provoked the guy in the Butterfly Saloon," said Bubba.

"No," snapped Wilkie, "*not* like that. That little snake spotted me before I knew he was there, and you saw what happened." In a softer tone, he continued, "But that brings up an important point. I've told you this before. So did Dick Wessell. When you have to confront one of the Joneses, or any man intending to use his gun, what's the most important thing to remember?"

"To get the drop," responded Dawkins.

"And what does that mean, Bubba?"

"It means I get my gun on him before he gets his on me."

"That's right, and it *don't* mean being faster on the draw or a better shot or any of that bullshit. We'll leave that up to Harris. What it *does* mean is, if you even think trouble is about to start, you get your gun on the man, right then. Sneak up on him, hide and wait for him, whatever it takes, but get your gun on him first." The sheriff leaned back in his chair. "And that," he said, "is the meaning of the drop."

Harris had looked up when his name was mentioned. He'd been listening to this dialogue and he felt somewhat reassured. There'd never been any question about Wilkie's competence, and thankfully, Bubba seemed willing to listen and learn. Placing both hands behind his neck, he asked: "Have you two forgotten about Snake River?"

"Nope," said the sheriff. "I've been thinking about him right along. Now we may have to wait for the brother's play, but Reese is wanted, so we can arrest him on sight." Eyeing Harris, he said, "Naturally, that's a problem all in itself."

"Yep, he just might object to that."

"Since he's wanted, he'll sneak in quietly, probably get here late at night, but he won't be far behind his nephews - or ahead of them."

Bubba took out a tobacco pouch and, folding a thin piece of paper, began to build a cigarette. "So how do we handle the uncle?"

"If you're talking about you and me," said the sheriff, "we don't, unless we happen to have a dead drop on him. One on one, Reese would kill you or me, and if we faced him together, he'd probably still get both of us. No, Reese is Harris's job. It's the real reason he's here. Of course, we'll back him if we can, but it'll probably come down to Harris and the gentleman from Snake River."

Bubba lit his cigarette, blew out smoke, and looked at the man on his right. Harris appeared deep in thought, head down, eyes half closed. As if feeling Bubba's gaze, he looked up and said, "I wouldn't have it any other way."

Charles Wilkie nodded in accord, but the notion running through his head was curiously similar to the sentiment Seth Jones had expressed by a lonely campfire several hours ago and many miles away. If I live to be a hundred, he thought, I'll never understand a gunfighter.

Chapter Three

Wednesday

The four men, with Bud in the lead, left the Ozark Mountains behind and were now riding across an expanse of low rolling hills. Bud noticed the sun had lowered in the west, but it still beat on him with unremitting heat and light, and the cloudless sky made the scene seem eternal. His canteen was empty as were the others, but this was green country and he knew that within these woods and grass, water would be found . Still, he and his companions had not wet their lips since mid-morning and their throats had become too dry for any talk that wasn't necessary. So they rode in silence, until Bud looked to his right and saw a clear stream bubbling below them. He pointed and gave a shout. Then they all saw it and he and James plunged down the hill, their horses shying clear of bushes and boulders. Bud reached the stream first, swung off his horse, and falling flat on his stomach, buried his face in the steam. He heard James splash down beside him, then glanced up to see Seth and Snake River Reese proceeding toward them at a walk. The boy lowered his face again, but before he could suck up more water, he felt a painful tug. He twisted around and there was Seth, kneeling between them, with both fists full of their hair. Lifting their heads he ordered, "Go loosen the cinches on your horses."

The horses drank downstream, bellies tight against the leather straps. Bud and James went over to loosen them, while Seth and Reese returned to their horses and did the same. After horses and men had drunk their fill, Bud tethered the mounts to a tree. James started a fire and put on coffee.

Reese looked around and then called out to his nephew, "Go ahead and unsaddle them, Bud. Set up a picket rope and let them graze. We'll camp here tonight."

Seth turned to him and said, "There's still some daylight left."

"I know, but the horses need to rest and so do we. Besides, it may be awhile before we run across another stream."

James poured coffee and said, "What day is it, Uncle Robert?"

"It's Wednesday, which means if we keep up the pace, we'll be in Medford sometime Friday night."

Sensing his uncle's relaxed mood, Bud said, "Seems like you know the sheriff pretty well, but have you ever met Henry Harris?"

Reese took a sip of coffee and his thin lips twisted in a sardonic smile. "Nope, unlike you boys, I've never had the pleasure, but I've heard all the talk."

"What have you heard, Uncle Robert?"

"Oh, the usual, about how fast he is and all."

Bud gave a shrug. "Yeah, they say that about most gunfighters."

"One old timer did tell me he'd never seen a cooler man

in a fight." Continuing to smile, Reese added, "This old geezer said you could reach out and rake the frost off him."

"You think all that's true?" asked Bud.

"Can't afford not to."

The cultivated gunman, still neat and clean-shaven after three days on the trail, rose and strolled down to the creek bank. He removed his hat and scarf, and with the latter washed his face and neck. On the way back, a startled rabbit burst from a clump of grass and sprinted up the hill. Reese's right hand flashed, the pistol in it thundered, and the rabbit turned a somersault and lay kicking in the grass. The Denver Gunfighter picked it up by the hind legs and returned to the campfire. Bud took the small animal from him and examined it. Reese's bullet had neatly taken its head off.

"I'll fix him up for supper," he muttered.

Later, the rabbit had been eaten, along with a pot of beans, and the men lazed around the fire. Reese slowly rolled a cigarette. Seth Jones puffed on a pipe.

The pipe smoker propped himself on an elbow and asked, "Robert, how the hell did you get that good?"

The gunfighter lit his cigarette from a burning twig. "Practice," he said.

"Well hell, me and the boys here practice. We've...I mean we could practice for a hundred years and...I guess what I'm gettin' at is you must know some kind of secret."

"No secret."

"Just practice?"

Snake River sat up and regarded his nephews, who were all watching him. Perhaps the family ties stirred him, or maybe it was just the rabbit and beans, still warm in his stomach, but suddenly he felt like making a response.

"Boys," he began, "it is not 'just practice' where you go out behind the barn to snatch and shoot for a bit. No, it's drawing and firing for, say, six hours every day, day after day, after day, practicing until your hand is numb and you're deaf from the gunshots."

The brothers all gawked at their uncle. None had ever heard him speak this way. And Bud, most perceptive of the three, said, "Why would a man give so much time to just one thing?"

Reese didn't hesitate. "To know that you're better at that 'one thing' than anyone else in the world."

The brothers continued to stare. Reese let his head drop and withdrew into himself. For awhile, there was no more talk around the campfire.

The setting sun spread a mellow light through the tree trunks and cast shadows across the creek. Reese rose, walked down to the water's edge, and continued along the creek bank. The immediate ground was soft and even, with a covering of moss, and his boots made no sound as he moved along. A soft breeze touched his face bringing the scent of muscadines, and a trout leaping in the brook drew the instant response of a dozen screeching tree frogs. The woods grew thicker and he paused beneath a prodigious oak tree, its branches reaching out across the narrow stream. A squirrel gave out a short bark and Reese caught sight of him, scampering along an upper limb. Another rapid motion, another explosive crash, and the small animal flew out from the tree limb and seem to fall in slow motion, his bushy tail streaming behind him. The gunfighter heard footsteps and saw Bud, coming through the trees. He handed over the squirrel. "Take him back and dress him for breakfast."

The young man started back, then paused. "You coming, Uncle Robert?"

"I'll be along in a minute," said Reese.

He remained standing under the oak, thinking about the

reason he was here. Seth had been right, of course. He had come to challenge Harris and soon they would meet. That was as inevitable as the coming darkness and the thought of it brought only a feeling of pleasant expectancy. Within Reese, there existed no self-doubt and certainly no fear. He was better. He was deadlier, and there could be only one outcome. The legend of Henry Harris was as great as his own, but that only increased Reese's anticipation. He hoped that his adversary was worthy, or in other words, that he would die well. And then he remembered what the old man had said about Harris, and he smiled as a mental magic lantern show formed in his head. In the show, that same old man was kneeling down and slowly brushing frost from Harris's lifeless shoulders.

The stranger rode into town on Wednesday night, horse and rider emerging at a slow walk out of the darkness. He had not been in Medford before and was looking for the livery stable. Spying it in the distance, he rode up and was dismounting when the stable boy came out.

"How much for the night?" he asked.

The stable boy took in the gaunt figure with the low-slung holster and said, "One dollar."

The dark man noted, with regret, a touch of apprehension on the young boy's face. "That include a rub down and forage?"

"Yessir," said the boy. "He'll get a rub down. Uh, what's forage?"

"Feed, boy, feed."

"Oh, yessir, he'll get that, too."

"Do you have a hotel in this town?"

"Yes sir, sure do. Kate's Place. Right on up the street and to your left."

The stranger lifted a cloth-wrapped package from his saddle bags and started to walk away. The boy called, "Mister, I need a name for the ticket."

"Murdock," the man said over his shoulder.

The boy led the buckskin into the stable and stripped off the saddle. Underneath lay a gray horse blanket with the letters CSA, stitched in faded red across the center. Another mystery. The boy understood the letters about as well as he understood forage.

The man called Murdock entered Kate's Place and walked to the counter. The black eyes widened slightly as he took in the woman behind it. Not only was she beautiful, with hair as dark as his and luminous brown eyes, but she exhibited the carriage and bearing of one of those aristocratic southern belles he had known so long ago. As a matter of fact she looked somehow familiar, but he could summon up no recollection. So many towns, so many hotels, so many saloons. If he'd met her before, it must have been many years back. The woman gazed back with no sign of recognition and Murdock dismissed it from his mind.

Kate nodded her head and said, "Good evening."

"Evening, ma'am. I'll be needing a room for the night."

"Just one night?"

"At the present, yes ma'am. I may need to stay longer, but I won't know that until tomorrow."

Kate took in the lean, almost emaciated frame, the chiseled face, and the cold, dark eyes. All that and the long, black hair hinted at Indian blood, but Katie wasn't fooled. The man before her, with the cultured manner and careful speech, was southern blue-blood if ever she saw it. You ran into them occasionally, refugees from the war, once proud owners of slaves and cotton land and pillared mansions. Now, disinherited and burnt out by battle, they had become wanderers, fortune hunters, and gunmen. However, this one seemed far from a burnt out case. It also seemed as though she'd seen that hawk-like face before, but not being sure, she gave no outward sign.

Katie picked up a pen, and sounding deferential in spite of herself, said, "I'll need your name, sir."

"The name is Murdock, ma'am, John Murdock."

Kate started to enter the name, but her pen stopped in mid-air. She looked up at Murdock and said, "Black Jack Murdock?"

"An unfortunate sobriquet, ma'am, but I confess I've been called that on occasion. It's owed to my appearance I suppose."

Katie entered the name, murmuring, "Before the war, I lived in Tishomingo County, not far from your plantation."

"Perhaps I saw you there," the man replied. And with a flash of the gallantry that went to his very marrow, he added, "Of course, you could not have been more than a girl at the time."

Kate smiled and bowed her head at the compliment. She found it easy to respond to this man, a figure from her homeland and her past. "I saw you on occasion, riding that great, black stallion of yours. I thought you had to be the handsomest man in Mississippi. I'm afraid I had a full-blown crush on you. It's an honor to meet you, sir."

Instantly, Murdock lifted his wide-brimmed hat and made a sweeping, floor skimming motion with it. Bowing deeply from the waist, he said, "The honor is entirely mine, Miss...?"

"Kate Mulroney," she informed him. "Those were good days, the days before the fighting."

"Indeed they were, ma'am. Very, ah, tranquil days."

Slipping easily into the mannered speech, she said, "I heard you met with some misfortune."

"Yes, I'm afraid I lost everything, even that black stallion you mentioned. As you may have heard, my wife died while I was serving in the Shenandoah. I was not permitted to come back for the funeral. After the war I returned to my land, but was unable to hold onto it. The reconstruction period was hard on all of us."

"Yes," she said, "I'm very sorry to hear about your loss."

"Well, Miss Mulroney, you know what they say. To the victor belong the spoils."

"I was thinking of your wife, sir."

"Yes, that loss was, of course, nearly unsustainable."

Kate nodded and said, "So what brings you to town, Mr. Murdock?"

"I'm afraid, madam, that I'm not at liberty to say, at least for the moment. However, after conferring with a certain gentleman tomorrow, I may be able to confide that information to you."

Kate, slightly flustered, said, "Oh, that won't be at all necessary, Mr. Murdock. I didn't mean to pry."

Murdock's black eyes softened for a moment. "May I call you Kate?"

"Of course."

"Well Kate, I don't mind telling you about it. After all, there should be no secrets between two former residents of Tishomingo County. However," he added, "to do so at the moment would betray a confidence."

"I understand," she said, handing Murdock a key. Your room is at the top of the stairs, first door on the left. I hope you rest comfortably."

Murdock bowed once more and headed up the stairs. Kate watched until he disappeared, then summoned an assistant from the dining room. The woman took her post behind the counter and Kate walked out the front door. She headed for the sheriff's office and almost collided with Bubba Dawkins.

"Bubba," she asked, "is the sheriff in his office?"

"Sure is, Kate."

"What about Harris? I haven't seen him all day."

"He's with the sheriff," said Bubba, and with a touch of pride, added, "Henry and me are taking turns with patrol."

Kate smiled and said, "Thank you, Bubba."

She entered the tobacco scented office and saw the men seated at a table. Two lamps, one on the table and one on Wilkie's desk, filled the office with a tawny glow and lit up both their faces. "Good Lord, Charlie," she exclaimed. "It's brighter in here at night than it is in the daytime."

The two men looked around and Wilkie exclaimed, "Well, I'll be damned. This is a rare privilege when one of the town's leading citizens pays a visit. Ain't that right, Henry?" Harris just nodded and smiled. Wilkie jumped to his feet and pulled out an empty chair. "Please have a seat, Miss Mulroney," he entreated. "I trust you'll find it comfortable, and that you'll overlook the wretched surroundings of my humble office."

Harris had to laugh. He'd never seen this old grouch play the role of roaring boy.

Katie sat down, a bemused expression on her face, as Wilkie continued: "Mr. Harris and I stand ready to hear and obey. Speak, please, and let us know your wishes."

Kate sighed and said, "Okay Charlie, give it a rest."

Wilkie chuckled and Harris asked, "What brings you over here, Katie?"

The hotel owner looked from one to the other. "There's someone at the hotel that you might find interesting. He just checked in."

"Who is it?" asked the sheriff.

"John Murdock," she answered

"Ahh," breathed Wilkie as he stretched his legs out and clasped both hands behind his head. His expression gave nothing away.

"You're talking about Black Jack Murdock," said Harris

"The very same. He's staying in room eleven."

Bubba Dawkins stepped through the open doorway and said, "Who's staying in room eleven? Is Reese here already?"

"Calm down, Bubba," said the sheriff. "It's too early for any of them to show."

Bubba came in and picked up the coffee pot. He poured a cup and asked, "Anybody want any?"

"Bring the pot over here and have a seat," said Wilkie.

Dawkins sat down and gave his companions a questioning look.

"Bubba," asked his boss, "have you ever heard of John Murdock, sometimes called Black Jack?"

"Oh, hell yeah, Charlie. Uh, excuse me, Kate. Why yeah, everybody's heard of Jack Murdock, at least everybody around here. He used to be one of the rich ones. Owned land over in Mississippi. Say, you used to live in that vicinity, didn't you Kate?"

"Yes," she answered. "What have you heard about him recently? I lead a sheltered life."

"Well, after he lost everything, he traveled out west for awhile. Did some prospecting. Worked as a deputy for a spell. Finally, I hear he put his gun up for hire and it didn't come cheap, main reason being that he's real good with it. He's been in several scrapes, but always come out on top. He's killed some men. Far as I know, he's still a hired gun."

"Or a soldier of fortune," added Wilkie.

"I like that better," said Kate.

"Anyway," said Bubba, "this particular soldier is

supposed to be some kind of dangerous. And it's said he'll use that gun for most any purpose, if the price is right."

"I've never heard of him doing anything against the law," said Wilkie.

"And what do you suppose he's doing here?" asked Harris.

"I asked what brought him to town," said Kate. "He told me he had to see somebody tomorrow. Said he'd let me know after that."

Wilkie gave her a quizzical look and she said, "Well, we *were* almost neighbors once."

Bubba was sipping his coffee. Suddenly he coughed and sat upright. "Sheriff, I just had a real bad thought," he said.

"What's that?"

"What if Murdock is here to join Reese and the Jones boys? What if they've bought his gun? That's five to three with two of 'em gunfighters. Bad odds."

"You thinking about resigning?" The sheriff gave him a bemused look.

Dawkins flushed and quietly said, "You know better than that, Sheriff Wilkie."

"Yes, I know better, Bubba. Just yanking your chain." That was as close as Wilkie would ever get to an apology. "Anyway," he continued, "Murdock would never join up with that bunch."

"What makes you so sure?" asked Kate.

"He'd consider himself their superior. And he'd be right."

Harris stirred himself and looked across the table. "That's all well and good, but Katie's got a point. How can you be so sure?"

Charles Wilkie gave them all a smug smile. "Because he came into town to see me. Hell, Harris, he's the other man I've been talking about."

* * *

Kate returned to the hotel counter and checked in seven more guests. That sold out ten rooms, which wasn't bad for a Wednesday night. Her hotel business had been steady from the beginning, each night would find most or all of the twelve rooms filled. And she did it without the benefit of saloon girls. At the very start, Kate decided that was a problem she didn't need and she'd never regretted the decision. Owning a hotel, a saloon, and a restaurant was headache enough. She didn't need the job of supervising a bunch of prostitutes. Certainly, none of the three enterprises had suffered from these "working girl's" absence. She listened to the din of the full saloon and the clinking dishes of a busy restaurant, and glanced at just two room keys remaining on the hooks behind her. Kate Mulroney had come a long ways.

Her parents had owned land in Tishomingo County, near the town of Duck Hill, Mississippi. The farm could have fit in a corner of the vast Murdock plantation, lying to the north, but the ground was fertile and the water plentiful. Most of it was given over to cattle, the remainder sown with wheat, alfalfa, and corn. They could not afford to grow cotton, the area's main money crop. That required a great amount of labor, and Thomas Mulroney, though not an abolitionist, refused to own a slave. He was, however, a sharp businessman and a shrewd investor, always aware of the favorable opportunity. He could also recognize ominous portents, or what he called "bad weather on the horizon". A full year before Fort Sumpter, he ceased all speculation, transferred his investments into gold certificates, and deposited them in a bank in St. Louis. The farm continued to provide an adequate living for them until the time of his death. That came three years later, when he succumbed to pneumonia. Within the month, Kate's mother died of the same hateful disease, struggling for breath and gripping the hand of her only child.

Kate was sixteen at the time. She was left alone, numb with shock and grief, but another misfortune awaited. She, too, contacted pneumonia, took to her bed, and for days lay insensible and uncaring. Then the raging fever abated, she began to breath more freely, and slowly she began her return to a familiar world. She heard a man's voice, and thinking back, Kate could hear it still, a sad and gentle voice, the sound of which had given her hope and comfort throughout the wretched illness:

"Ah, Katherine, ye had us all worried, but ye've come out of it fine."

Her lips twitched in a smile and she murmured, "Uncle Eric?"

"Right the first time," he said. "But how did ye guess?"

Kate opened her eyes, gazed fondly at her uncle, and in a teasing tone said, "Now, Eric Mulroney, would ye be askin' that of another one of the Irish, and your own niece, besides?"

Mulroney had gathered her wasted form into his arms and Kate wept. She'd never wept since, but on that day, she shuddered and sobbed and cried out against all that had befallen her. Her uncle held her in a silent embrace, and unknown to Kate Mulroney, he was weeping, too. Eric's wife, who'd arrived with her husband, watched from the open doorway. She dabbed at her eyes and walked back to the kitchen.

Eric Mulroney was older than his brother, and unlike him, was born in Ireland. Their mother was pregnant with Thomas when they got off the boat. After they grew up, both brothers, always close, traveled to Mississippi and began their respective trades. Eric became a cotton broker and Thomas began to farm. Through hard work and intelligent planning, both the brothers prospered. Now, entering the third year of war, their enterprises had suffered as the whole South had suffered. Much worse lay ahead.

When Kate was up and about, she asked her Aunt and Uncle if they could stay for awhile. Both agreed. Eric became a sort of farm manager and Aunt Eunice tended the chickens, milked the cows, and helped keep house. As Katie grew stronger, she began to think and plan. One morning, around the breakfast table, they all three had a talk. Katie led things off.

"Uncle Eric," she began. "I want to leave the farm."

After the initial uproar, a final plan emerged. Eric, who's brokerage business had been done in by the war, would take over the farm and continue to run it. He and Eunice would keep all the proceeds, little enough in view of the looming holocaust, and Katie would move to St. Louis, where her grandparents lived. There were good schools there, a growing economy, and, though she didn't say it, a chance to be on her own.

So it had all come to pass. She was in St. Louis when the war ended. A Reconstruction government took the farm and there was nothing her uncle could do about it. They gave him a small settlement. He offered it to Katie, but she told him to keep it. He returned to the brokerage business and eventually regained a livelihood. Now, he and Aunt Eunice were dead. And the farm, which the Yankee government had never made any use of, was gone to scrub land and waste, home to rabbits and deer and the moaning wind.

Kate attended school, grew up, took lovers, and buried her grandparents. She eventually married a lawyer named Simmons. They never had any children, and several years later the marriage ended in an amicable divorce, amicable because Katie refused any financial support. She didn't really need any. Her father's gold certificates had always been there, steadily increasing in value. Katie had dipped into them a few times over the years, but the majority remained. It was enough to realize her plan. Katie would head back into a new South and start her own business. She traveled down the Mississippi, disembarking at the town of Medford, Arkansas, and there she began a new life. An old, neglected, two-story building stood on Medford's main street. It had once been a hotel. Katherine would make it one again. Remodeled and virtually rebuilt, it arose from its own remains and became Kate's Place. A restaurant and saloon were eventually added and all were improved upon over the years. These feats, of course, had not been accomplished without a world of sacrifice and setbacks and hardships. Now, as Katherine Mulroney stood behind the hotel counter and ran her hand across the woodwork, she felt she hadn't done too badly.

Her reverie was interrupted by the sound of boots on the stairs. She looked up and saw John Murdock descending. He approached her and removed his hat, which, along with his clothing, had been carefully brushed.

"You look lovely this evening, Miss Kate," he proclaimed.

Kate gave a small curtsey. "Why, thank you, Mr. Murdock." She wanted to confess to him what she knew, but didn't quite know how to go about it.

Murdock leaned forward from the waist, and in a conspiratorial tone, asked, "How did the sheriff respond?"

Katie felt a sudden weakness in the knees. "Respond to what?"

"Why, to your information, dear lady. Your information about me."

Kate recovered and said, "Yes, I went to see him, but how did you know?"

"Murdock smiled and replied, "Well, I didn't know for

sure, but I knew you two were friends. Charlie told me so. And what else would a friend of the sheriff's do when that person came across a piece of information that might be, ah, useful to him?"

"You're very astute, sir."

Black Jack inclined his head, smiled, and said, "Apart from the Tishomingo days, what do you know about me? That is to say, what have you heard?"

"I heard you fought gallantly in the war, that you were with General Lee at Appomattox, and that now you've become... " she borrowed Wilkie's words, "...a soldier of fortune."

"A high-flying description for someone who is, in fact, a hired gun."

"I do not believe you let it be hired indiscriminately, sir."

The smile widened and Murdock said, "I think I'll join that assemblage behind the swinging doors."

"Katie returned the smile and said, "Are you in need of their company, Mr. Murdock?"

"No ma'am," he answered, "but I am in need of a drink."

Murdock had started away when Kate called, "Will you help the sheriff?"

He stopped, half turned, and said, "There is that possibility. Good night, Miss Kate."

Katie watched him pass through the swinging doors and murmured to herself, "I sure hope so. You're exactly the help Charlie needs."

Chapter Four

Thursday

Harris awoke early on Thursday morning, and found that Katie had already left his bed. He settled back against a feather pillow and allowed himself to think about her. And Kate Mulroney was a woman who inspired some thought. They'd known each other for over ten years, first meeting in the sheriff's office when she'd come over to bail out her dishwasher on a drunk and disorderly charge. Harris was the deputy and he'd walked her back to the hotel. From the first moment, she'd seemed like someone he'd always known and they had talked and talked. From that beginning, a lasting bond was formed and they came to be lovers, helpmates, and confidantes. They knew all about each other's pasts, and with that knowledge came mutual respect. Theirs was a wonderful friendship and a great alliance, but Henry didn't see how it could come to anything more. "Different worlds," they'd both said, and both of them were right.

Sunlight streamed through the curtains and lit up tiny dust motes, hanging and drifting in the air. Harris flung back the covers, a rueful look on his face. He never slept this late on the farm, always up before daylight. He splashed water on his face and leered at himself in the mirror. That's right, he thought. But on the farm a bed was used only for sleeping. Here, it served an additional purpose, and Katie was a very attentive lover, attentive and active. With a wry smile, Harris thought that if Kate *did* live with him, there'd be a lot of late awakenings.

He dressed and went downstairs. Kate's assistant, a girl named Kerrie, was stationed behind the counter, collecting room payment from a guest. Harris walked into the restaurant and took a table. Marge Blackwell, the restaurant supervisor, came over with a menu.

"How've you been, Margie?" he said, taking the menu from her.

"Not bad, Mr. Harris. How 'bout yourself?"

"Pretty good." Harris hated small talk. "Where's your boss?"

"Had to go out to the Potter farm to pick up some poultry and produce. She should be back by noon."

Harris's eyes were drawn to a lanky stranger sitting in the corner. His felt hat rested on the table and the black hair, combed straight back, hung long and loose. The dark, somber eyes gazed off into the distance. The man sat erect, hands on the table and both feet flat on the floor. He took a sip of coffee, glanced at Harris, and slowly inclined his head. Harris gave a return nod and said to the waitress, "Margie, let's hold off on the order for a minute. I'm going to speak to that gentleman in the corner. If I sit down, you can bring the menu over there. Otherwise, I'll come back here and order."

"Sure thing," said Margie."

"By the way, do you know the gentleman's name?"

"Yep, Miss Kate told me. It's Jack Murdock. I always thought he was a gunman, but Miss Kate said he was a first class gentleman."

"Well, Miss Kate is usually right," said Harris.

He got up and walked to the corner table. The man seated there continued to sip his coffee and gaze into the distance, but his right hand left the table and found a place on the chair seat, just beside the pistol.

Harris, summoning up an attempt at manners, said, "Excuse me, but I wonder if I might join you."

The lean face turned toward him and Harris could almost hear a click when the black eyes locked onto his. The dark man studied Harris for a moment, then rose and extended his hand. "A pleasure, sir," he murmured.

Harris sat in the opposite chair and said, "I do believe I'm addressing Mr. John Murdock." The words came out formally, but how could you not be formal with this man?

The man nodded and replied, "I'm afraid you have the advantage of me, sir."

"The name is Harris, Henry Harris."

"Ahh," breathed Murdock, "the sheriff's friend, and I suppose you're now his deputy." After a slight pause, he added, "In addition to your other vocation."

"Well yes. I also own a farm."

"I was not aware of that," said Black Jack.

Harris's eyes narrowed. "What 'other vocation' are you aware of, sir?"

"Why your reputation speaks for itself," said Murdock, leaning back in his chair, both hands back on the table. "My goodness, Mr. Harris. I'm just a poor Mississippi boy, who had to go away to the war, but even I have heard of your, ah ...achievements."

"That was quite a while back. I've been a farmer for ten years. I'm surprised you remember the other."

"Oh, many people remember, sir. Not the least of which are the Jones brothers."

"I'm afraid that's true," said Harris. He was not about to ask Black Jack if he intended to take a hand. That should be left to Charlie Wilkie.

"Besides," continued Murdock, "your activities in the past were somewhat similar to mine. I like to keep an eye on my fellow players."

"And your own reputation is not unknown to me, sir." Why am I continuing to talk this way, he wondered. He was certainly no southern gentleman. But Murdock brought it out in a man. He felt compelled to respond in his language. What a fiendish gift.

"I served to the best of my ability," Murdock was saying, "but I did no more than many of my compatriots."

"I was talking about after the war."

Murdock stared at him. "Well, after the war, I was obliged to seek another occupation."

"What part of the war were you in, Mr. Murdock?"

"Oh, many parts." A quick smile. "All on the southern side, of course. I had the honor of serving with General Jackson in the Shenandoah. After Jackson's death, I became a colonel in Jeb Stuart's cavalry and remained there until General Lee's surrender. And what about you, sir?"

"Well," said Harris, "I'm afraid I never got any higher than sergeant. And I was too young to see much of the war. I got in near the end and soldiered with General Hood."

"An estimable man," said Murdock, "but rash...rash."

Margie came over and Harris ordered bacon and eggs. Murdock looked at her and shook his head.

"You're not eating, Mr. Murdock?"

"No, I seldom eat breakfast, Mr. Harris, and do not eat much at other times. My poor stomach was a casualty of the war. Too much hardtack and fatback, I suppose."

Murdock drained his coffee and daintily wiped his lips with a napkin. He rose and said, "Now, if you'll excuse me, sir, I have an appointment to see the sheriff."

Harris nodded and Murdock had started away when a raised voice came from the adjoining table, "One of 'em's leaving, Dan. We won't have to listen to no more rebel bullshit."

Harris twisted around and recognized the source, a government land agent, who'd checked in the same time as he. The man had a burly build with the promise of a paunch swelling against his belt buckle. A local lawyer, Daniel Morris, sat with him.

Murdock had an ungraceful walk, the long, thin legs hinging and unhinging like a clasp knife. He reached the agent's table, paused, and looked down at him. Harris could plainly see the smoldering eyes.

"Was that remark directed at me, sir?"

The heavyset man stood up and regarded the skinny stranger. He grinned. "Damn right, and it came from a former first sergeant in the army of General Sherman."

Several other customers, frowning and hard-eyed, had already risen from their chairs. Margie Blackwell, seeing and hearing all, made a dash to the table and yelled at the agent, "You danged fool, do you want to die? There's a room full of southerners here, and you just insulted Black Jack Murdock."

The loudmouth took a step backward and sweat sprung out on his face. He fished for a handkerchief, but never got a chance to use it. In a movement as fluid and graceful as his walk had been stilted and awkward, Black Jack drew his sidearm and whipped it sideways against the salesman's head. The man crumpled to his knees and remained there, blood pouring from his scalp and running down his collar. Murdock turned to the man's open-mouthed companion and said,

"Better get him out of here before some of these gentlemen finish the job."

Morris pulled the bleeding man to his feet and hustled him out the door. Harris turned back to his coffee and John Murdock continued on his way. He did not look back or give any recognition to the multiple clapping of hands.

Harris finished his breakfast and stepped up to the counter. He smiled at Margie and said, "You did good. That was quick thinking. And quick acting."

Margie shook her head and said, "I couldn't believe it at first. Guy must have had a death wish. This is a southern town."

"Well," said Harris, "old war wounds run deep."

Marge chuckled. "I thought he was gonna choke when I told him who he was talking to. Didn't dare mention your name. He might've had a seizure."

Harris replaced his hat and said, "I'll be at the sheriff's office if anybody happens to ask."

Margie's plump face broke into a grin and she said, "When Miss Anybody comes in, I'll tell her."

Harris stepped out into a day threatened by storm. Billowing, black clouds were approaching from the west and a fresh wind brought the smell of rain. Two horseman trotted toward the livery stable, anxious to arrive before the storm broke. Harris gave them a close look, then saw that they were locals. Both men dismounted, tied their horses, and entered the stable. The horses stood patiently, tails blowing between their legs. Harris hurried toward the sheriff's office. He was fifteen feet away when, drops of rain began spattering into the street, raising dusty puffs and leaving dark splotches of moisture. The scent of rain became stronger, and as he entered the office, the deluge began, rattling down on the building's tin roof. Harris suddenly thought about Kate and wondered if she was caught out in the weather.

* * *

Charlie and John Murdock were standing next to the wall, gazing at the poster on Snake River Reese.

"You've seen him since I have," said Wilkie. "Is this a good likeness?"

Murdock continued to study the sketch. "Not bad. Actually quite accurate as these drawings go."

The sheriff turned to Harris. "You might want to take a final look at this."

Harris walked over and glanced at the poster. "What do you mean, 'final look'?"

Wilkie ripped off the poster, crumpled it up, and returned to the table. The other two men joined him and everyone took a chair. "I mean," said Charlie, "that Robert Reese is no longer a wanted man."

Harris just stared and the sheriff continued: "Snake River killed a man out in the Oklahoma Territory, fellow known as Moose Barton. Two witnesses swore it was done in cold blood and a warrant was issued along with these posters. Then, three other men came forward and swore it was a clear case of self-defense. After that, the first two men reversed their statements and said it could have been self-defense after all. So the charges were dropped and the posters recalled. Now, Snake River is just another citizen."

"It would have been much easier to deal with him as a fugitive," stated Murdock. "We could have arrested him on sight. Now we have to wait for his play."

"Yeah," said the sheriff, "we've already discussed that."

Harris considered the gaunt figure. "So you've decided to throw in."

Murdock gave a slight nod of acknowledgment and turned to the sheriff. "Mr. Harris is a man of rare restraint.

We spent some time together and not once did he ask me what my decision would be."

"Maybe he already knew."

"I doubt it. Since I did not know myself, before talking to you."

The sheriff frowned and said, "Do you mind telling me what the hell I said that finally swayed you?"

"Oh nothing, Charlie, nothing at all. I just wanted to make sure you had retained that same old lovable nature."

Harris gave a soft chuckle. "I think Mr. Murdock first wanted to see the situation for himself."

John Murdock pulled a dark brown cheroot from his pocket, lit up, and blew out a thin stream of smoke. "That's true, Mr. Harris, but my feeling about Charlie is, to an extent, also true. You see, he controls the situation. Had he become, ah, altered, I may have rode on."

"You mean, if I had gotten soft," grumped the sheriff. "Well, I'm just real glad I passed your muster."

It was Murdock's turn to chuckle. "You did, Charlie. You did indeed."

Harris said, "I take it you two go back a ways."

"Well," said Charlie, "I haven't seen Jack in eleven or twelve years, but we've done a few things together, stole some horses, as they say."

"An unfortunate phrase, Charlie. Actually, we were always on the right side of the law. As a matter of fact, we were deputies together in Denver. He rendered me some assistance there, as I recall."

"Saved your ass is what I recall. And more than once," said the sheriff.

Everyone laughed and Harris asked, "Did Mr. Murdock ever return the favor?"

Wilkie gazed at the ceiling and said, "Seems like the

rain is letting up." No one replied, and he finally growled, "Oh, hell yes. Are you happy now?"

Murdock and Harris wore grins and the sheriff scowled at both of them. "And another thing, how long are you two gonna keep up this 'Mr.' business? You sound like a couple of damn lawyers."

John Murdock straightened and the black eyes studied Harris. He slowly stretched out his hand and said, "My friends call me Jack."

Harris did not take the moment lightly. In the same solemn way, he took the offered hand and said, "It's an honor, Jack. My friends just call me Harris."

"Wilkie watched them while he filled his clay pipe. When he'd packed and tamped the tobacco to his satisfaction, he lit up and leaned back. Glancing at Murdock, he said, "Okay, what's your view?"

"The man to watch is Reese," said Jack. "He is, of course, the most dangerous. I'm wondering if he knows the warrant has been lifted."

"He might," said Wilkie. "If so, he'll ride in bold as brass. If not, he'll come in on the sly."

"You sure?" asked Harris. "From what I've heard, Reese ain't the one for sneaking around."

Wilkie made no reply and Murdock said, "Charlie is being modest. The so-called Denver Gunfighter knows the sheriff would do his job."

"So you're both acquainted with Reese."

"Charlie and I encountered the gentleman on two or three occasions," said Murdock, "all in the city of Denver. Words were passed, but it never came down to guns, maybe because it was two against one."

Wilkie said, "We arrested his ass twice. Once for violating the gun ordinance and once for threatening a bartender. Before he left town, Reese came over to the jail and said he hoped he'd see each of us in some other place. Said he was really looking forward to meeting us one at a time. I don't believe he was speaking out of fellowship."

"Did either of you ever see him after that?"

"Jack did," said Wilkie. "He was passing through . . . What was the name of that town, Jack?"

"It doesn't come to mind," replied Murdock. "Somewhere over in east Kansas."

"Anyway, Jack caught sight of him in a saloon, sitting at a poker table."

"What happened?" asked Harris.

"Tell him, Jack," said the sheriff.

Murdock puffed on the cigar and said, "Well, upon noticing Mr. Reese, I was immediately filled with curiosity, so I walked over and asked him if we had any unfinished business. He informed me that we did, but that it would keep until a later date."

"So he backed down," said Harris.

"Well," said Black Jack, "it would be gratifying to think so, but I noticed there was a great deal of money piled in front of him. I believe he was simply unwilling to break off from a winning streak."

"Okay," said Charlie. "Let's get back to business."

The three men huddled over the table and Henry Harris glanced at the dark stranger, who had now become his friend. There, he thought, sits a very dangerous man.

The four men had approached Little Rock from the north. One of them entered the town. The others swung toward the east and were now sitting around a late night campfire, where

James had prepared a scanty supper. He was carrying all their food and coffee in his saddlebags and both food and coffee were almost gone. What, he wondered, were they going to do when the bags were empty. A clear stream running close by, had induced them to stop here, and tonight, water was plentiful. Also, it was close to where their uncle had left them and only five miles from town, so he shouldn't have any trouble finding them again.

James stirred the fire and said, "I still don't get it. Robert said no towns and now he's smack in the middle of a big one. Little Rock must have twenty lawmen."

"Your uncle knows what he's doing," said Seth.

"Maybe so," said James, "but what the Sam Hill *is* he doing?"

"James and I figured he might've told you," added Bud.

Seth stroked his beard. "Well, if you're so all-fired hot to know, he's using the telegraph."

"To do what?" asked Bud.

"He's wiring Denver. Your uncle thinks the murder charges might've been dropped. He's got a friend there who can tell him."

James looked puzzled. "Why on earth would he think that?"

"He didn't confide that to me," said Seth, "but knowing Robert, he's probably got good reason to think so."

Suddenly, from up the hill a ways, came a familiar voice. "Hello, the camp."

Bud jumped up and yelled, "It's us, Uncle Robert."

Horse and rider came within the firelight and Snake River Reese dismounted. He looked at the youngest Jones and said, "Bud, would you get his saddle off and give him some water? And bring those saddle bags over here"

"Sure, Uncle Robert," the lad replied, and led the horse away.

James stared at Reese, thinking he looked unusual. Then, it occurred to him what it was. The man was wearing a smile.

Seth was also examining his uncle. "I take it you got some good news."

"Yep, the man I talked to happens to be the telegraph station manager. Late last night, the sheriff in Denver sent out a telegram. It said, as near as I can recall, that 'the charge of murder against one Robert Reese, known as Snake River Reese, has been hereby rescinded and Mr. Reese is no longer sought on this charge. If you have in your possession any handbills relating to this warrant, you will destroy them immediately."

"You knew this might happen," said Seth. "I figure you got some of your pals to go to the judge and swear it was self defense."

Reese peered at the oldest nephew. "You know, Seth. You may be smarter than I thought."

Seth smiled and Reese continued, "Of course, my pals also had to convince those original two yahoos that they'd seen the same thing."

Bud returned with Reese's saddlebags and the gunfighter brought out beans, bacon, and coffee. Also, half a ham and a dozen pieces of corn pone. Bud eyed the food, whistled softly, and said. "Time to eat again. What we had before couldn't rightly be called supper." Soon, part of the larder was cooked and eaten by the hungry men.

Reese swallowed a final spoonful of beans and wiped his lips with a faded bandanna. "We've got about ninety miles to go. We'll start before daylight and stay in the saddle all day. That'll put us in Medford sometime after dark."

"Then it's time to do a little planning," said James.

"Yes, I believe it is."

Bud edged closer to the fire and fixed his uncle with a

stare. The firelight lent a blood-red gleam to his eyes and gave him a feral look. "Before we start, let's have a final understanding."

The young man's serious and forthright demeanor startled his two brothers, but Snake River Reese merely shrugged.

"What is it, Bud?" he asked.

"We kill 'em all," said the youngest of the Jones brothers. "We shoot that sheriff and his deputy and that damn gunfighter, Harris. And, if we can round up a couple of them pus-bellied jurors, we gun them too."

For a moment, all was quiet around the campfire. Then Robert Reese quietly answered him. "That's what we came for, Bud."

James got to his feet and said, "Bud's right. They got it coming, every damn one of 'em, for what they did to us."

Seth rose up beside him and stood looking down at Reese. "Robert, I reckon you probably know more than us about a lot of things, but you ain't never been inside a prison. Ten years," he exclaimed. "Ten years, and nobody but us knows what we had to do, what we had to endure. And they won't know, because we'll never tell it all. We'd be too ashamed." He looked down at his youngest brother. "And Bud had it the worst."

Both men resumed their seats and Seth added, "Don't you worry, Bud. We'll gun 'em and gut 'em. You can depend on it."

Bud scooted backward and turned away from the campfire. In the flickering shadows, he still looked like a kid. "Good," they heard him murmur. "That's good."

Reese recognized the hatred and knew how to take advantage of it. "Okay," he said, "that's the kind of talk I like. I feel better now, and it's not because the law is off my back." He leaned forward and said, "You know why I feel better? Because I see three men with a purpose. We're together and we're family, and those bastards we're after are all dead men." Reese paused, for a moment, and added, "So gather round boys and let's talk." The men leaned closer and Bud came in from the dark and joined them.

"There's one thing for sure," said the sheriff, "they ain't just gonna ride into town and trust to luck. They'll have something figured out."

"With Reese leading them," said Murdock, "I'd say that's a fair assumption."

Harris said, "Seth Jones is no fool either. As a matter of fact, I wouldn't underestimate any of them. The brothers work well together. I don't think killing will faze them much, and they're all pretty good with a gun. Of course, no need to even talk about Snake River."

Jack Murdock looked at Harris and said, "You and Charlie have dealt with the Joneses before."

Harris said, "Yeah, and that's the reason we're having to deal with them again. They didn't like what we did to 'em, and I do believe those boys share a vengeful spirit."

"It might be of benefit to us," said Jack, "if you would recount your experiences."

"Maybe so," said Charlie, "but Dawkins should hear it, too. He's across the street at the barber shop." He stood up, saying, "I'll be back in a minute."

Harris and Murdock were left alone to contemplate each other. Neither man spoke for awhile, Black Jack puffing on his cigar and Harris sipping coffee.

Harris grinned at Murdock and said, "Did anybody ever see a dead cavalryman?"

Murdock's black eyes flicked to his and the thin lips twitched in a smile. "Fighting words, sir. But, as you know, that was an expression used in the Yankee infantry."

"Did you ever meet Jeb Stuart?"

"I was denied that honor. Shortly before I 'jined the cavalry', as they say, General Stuart was killed at Yellow Tavern. That's one dead cavalryman we can count."

Harris realized it was dangerous to address a teasing remark to this man, but Jack's demeanor and way of speaking made it difficult to resist. He realized he liked this formal southerner a great deal. "I understand you also served with Stonewall Jackson," he said.

"Yes, I was with him during the Valley campaign. I was only a major so I didn't meet him more than half a dozen times."

"He's coming to be known as a military genius."

"Oh, he was that," said Murdock, "but I sometimes believed him mad."

"I've heard he had some ways."

"He rode around with his right hand raised above his head. I had no idea why until General Ewell told me. Seems Stonewall thought he had too much blood in his right extremity and that it needed to drain back down, or something like that."

The two men talked on about the war until Wilkie returned with Bubba Dawkins in tow. Dawkins was wiping shave cream from his chin and giving Black Jack a curious look.

Both sat down and Wilkie said, "Bubba, I want you to meet John Murdock. John, this is my deputy, Bubba Dawkins."

Bubba extended his hand. Jack took it and murmured, "An honor, sir."

Dawkins positively beamed. "Mr. Murdock, I guess everybody's heard of you."

"Well, the war's over, I'm afraid."

"No sir, I mean from after the war.

Black Jack Murdock sighed.

"Jack's agreed to help us with our troubles," said Wilkie.

"So," said Bubba. "we got Henry Harris and Black Jack Murdock. Uh, sorry, Mr. Murdock."

"Quite all right," said Jack. "You may call me Jack if I can call you . . .ah, do you prefer Bubba or your given name?"

"Whichever suits you, Mr. . . . I mean Jack. My given name is Horace."

"Nice to meet you, Bubba," replied Murdock.

Everyone chuckled and Wilkie asked, "How do you see them coming in, Jack?"

"If our friend, Reese, learns he's no longer wanted, they may come in together. He'll figure that will intimidate a lone sheriff and his deputy."

Bubba slapped his leg and said, "Wait'll they see that we're backed up by you two."

The sheriff glanced at his deputy. Here was no coward, he thought, but Bubba's relief was evident. He was like a man saved from drowning. He cleared his throat and said, "That brings up a point that's already been discussed. When the action starts, things will be confused. They always are, and we'll have to adapt and do what's necessary. "But," he said, eyeing Harris and Murdock, "since these two are the, uh . . ."

"Deadliest," proclaimed Kate Mulroney. She came in bearing a pot of coffee and a pan full of ginger bread. Placing the items on the table, she said, "I'll leave you to your work."

She was almost to the door when Murdock called, "Appreciated, Miss Kate." Without turning around or slowing down, Katie lifted a hand and disappeared out the doorway.

"A woman of great quality," he said. The other three nodded.

"Anyway," said the sheriff, "we'll try to remain together. But Reese might try to set up a one on one. If that happens, and if it's possible, the man facing Reese needs to be Murdock or Harris."

"I agree," said Murdock, "but I believe this is the time to be frank with one another. No ego or false pride." He nodded toward Harris. "Between this man and myself, he's no doubt better with a gun, probably a great deal better."

Henry started to protest but Black Jack raised his hand and continued, "Oh, I've heard enough reliable reports to believe it, Harris. Anyway, it's just something we should be clear on."

"Okay," said Wilkie. "When do you think they'll get here?"

"My guess is tomorrow night," said Harris. "They'll push to make it so as not to camp out again. Sleeping on the hard ground gets old after a while."

"Yeah," said Wilkie, "their first stop will be the livery stable and then Kate's Place. I'm thinking we won't have to deal with them until Saturday."

"I believe Charlie is right," said Jack. "The next day is when they'll come at us."

Wilkie nodded and Murdock continued, "Now, I think that, when that next day comes, we should press them a little bit. After all, we know they've come for us. Why wait for them to choose the time and place?" He looked from one to the other. "I'm not saying initiate an immediate showdown, just nudge them a little bit. See how they react. See how smart they are. They might even break a law."

The sheriff sighed and said, "Well, I imagine you're the

best at doing that, Jack." He looked around and asked, "Y'all feel the same way?"

Both men nodded and Wilkie said, "Just remember, when Black Jack does the nudging, we need to be real close. Now, anybody got anything else to offer?"

Bubba held up a hand, which Wilkie regarded with a slight smile. "Yes, Bubba."

The young deputy hitched his chair forward. "What if we've got our times a little wrong and they come in tonight. We'll get caught by surprise."

Wilkie frowned and said, "Didn't you hear what Harris said? There's no..."

Harris cleared his throat and spoke softly. "That wouldn't be possible, Bubba. We know how they're traveling, when they started, and where they started from. Friday night is the earliest they could be here."

The young man nodded, and Charlie said, "Okay, we'll get to do some more planning later. Anything else till then?"

There was a moment of silence and Murdock said, "It appears not. Now why don't you two tell me and Bubba how all this ruckus got started?"

Wilkie fished a sack of tobacco from his shirt pocket and refilled his pipe. He lit the contents with a long kitchen match and said, "A little over ten years ago, I was elected sheriff of Phillips County. A short while after that, I took on Dick Wessell as my deputy. It didn't take long to find out that Dick was a solid man, because, right at the first, we ran into trouble. One of the Jones brothers, James Jones, was in town one Saturday night and commenced causing problems. He got drunk and pistol whipped the clean-up boy in Kate's Saloon. Then he started riding up and down main street, firing his pistol in the air and cussing a blue streak. Dick went out with a rifle, and when James rode by him, he used it like a bat and swatted him right off his horse. Well, Jones jumped up and fumbled for his gun and Dick poleaxed him again with the rifle." Wilkie chuckled. "That boy's head must have been made outta cast iron 'cause he jumped up a second time and him and Dick Wessell locked up. Well, to make a long story short, Dick just beat the bejesus out of Jones. I don't know whether it was Wessell's fists or the two swings with the rifle that done it, but James wound up with a broken nose, two black eyes, and a whole bunch of cuts and bruises. And, oh yeah, a couple of broken ribs. I reckon that had to be the rifle. Anyway, Dick hauled him off to jail, and there he sat for a whole week before the family came looking for him."

"Yeah, I've heard a lot of stories about that family," said Bubba.

"Well," said Charlie, "I don't know about all the stories, but the Jones bunch was nothing but bad news. Back then, the daddy, Old Man Lucius, was still alive. The mama was dead and the old man and the three boys lived alone in a log cabin up in the hills. They hunted and fished and trapped to get by. All this seemed harmless enough, but a lot of rumors started circulating. Tales about robberies, kidnappings, and killings up in the hills. Now the hill people are a close knit bunch, none of them were about to press charges, but the Jones name kept cropping up. Then the bank got robbed over in Walnut Grove. The robbers got away, but they were described as 'one old man, two younger men, and a boy.' That sure sounded like the Jones clan, so Dick and I went out and brought 'em in. They came peacefully, which surprised me, but it all come to naught. The robbers had worn kerchiefs and hats pulled down over their eyes, so nobody could positively identify them. Or," he continued, "maybe the victims were just too scared. Anyway, the old man and his sons got drunk, had a good laugh about it, and went on back to their cabin. Of course, I'm sure they didn't appreciated being hauled into town in the first place. And they weren't the kind to forget."

The sheriff's pipe had gone out. He placed it on the table, and said, "So now, it's back to where I left off, and the Old Man, Seth, and Bud have come into town to pay the fine and pick up Brother James. When they saw him in the cell, they pitched a fit. Actually, James didn't look as bad as he had at first. The doctor had bandaged his ribs and patched him up, but I guess he still looked kinda rough. Anyway, the Old Man wanted to know who done this, said if he found out, he'd shoot him on sight. Dick was standing off to one side. He reached up and took down a shotgun and covered them with it. I knew what he was about to say, so I jumped in ahead of him. 'The law did this, I said, and if you don't start showing a little more respect, that same law is gonna lock you up with young James here.' Well, they paid the fine and lit out, but I'll tell you, boys, there was murder in their eyes that day. Dick and I both knew we hadn't heard the last from the Jones bunch."

Outside, the rain had stopped and a cool breeze wafted through the open doorway. A lone horseman trotted past, the horse's hooves throwing back spatters of mud. Charlie relit his pipe and continued, "So several months rolled by. We kept looking over our shoulders for the Jones clan, but they stayed away and everything was quiet"

He glanced at Harris and said, "However, during that time, two interesting things did happen. Number one: Henry Harris rode into town, and number two: Kate Mulroney bought an old rundown building and named it Kate's Place."

"It wasn't my first time here," said Harris, "but it was the first time I'd met up with the sheriff." He smiled at Wilkie. "Charlie gave me a little talk."

"What did he say?" asked Bubba.

"I told him," said Charlie, "that whether he realized it or not, he was a danger to the peace of this county because he was a man with a reputation. I think he realized it, but I honestly don't think he knew how big that reputation was. Before Harris left town, he had cause to find out. Anyway, our boy here, was understanding enough. He'd been doing some bounty hunting and was on the trail of a man named Pat Whiteside. I knew the skunk and gave Henry some information about his whereabouts. Was it helpful, Henry? I never asked you."

"Yes, it was," replied Harris.

"Harris left two days after that. He came back through in about a week and his timing couldn't have been better."

"But what happened before he left town," asked Bubba.

The sheriff, lost in his story, gave Bubba a blank stare.

"You said that Harris would find out how big his repu—"

"Oh, yeah. It wasn't a real big deal. Wessell wanted Harris, here, to give him a few lessons. I never thought I'd hear Dick Wessell ask anyone for instructions on how to handle a gun, but Harris agreed and they went out behind the livery stable to practice. Well, what with the gunshots, it didn't take long for a few people to gather, and when they found out Harris was there, it became a crowd. I noticed what was happening and walked over. Henry and Dick had set up some ginger ale bottles on a fence. They stood about twenty-five feet away and Henry drew at a normal speed, letting his pistol barrel swing up and pop off a round. Of course, each time he did that, a bottle exploded. All the time, I could hear him talking to Wessell.

'Don't hurry,' he'd say, 'and keep your speed constant. The more you practice, the faster you'll get, but right now, just remember that from the time your hand starts to move until the round is fired, the speed should stay the same,' and so on. And he'd say, 'Accuracy is most important, but you got no problem there.' Then he'd demonstrate again and say, 'Don't stiffen the right hand. It has to stay flexible.'

I'd started to get interested myself, along with the crowd, when I noticed two strangers coming around the building. Both were young and wearing flashy clothes, but only one wore a sidearm. And only one of them walked with a swagger. You can guess which one that was. So they stood a ways off and the one that was heeled looked at his partner and said in a loud voice, 'Are you sure that dude is Harris?'

The other one nodded his head and the pop-off said, 'Well, hell, if he ain't no faster than that, maybe I should give him lessons."

Wilkie paused and shook his head. "I couldn't believe the idiot. He actually had it in his fool head that this was Henry's normal draw. Well, everything got real quiet and I started toward the strangers, but Henry already saw the solution. He'd been reloading his gun and slowly continued, paying no mind to the heckler. When he finished, he dropped the gun into the holster and stood facing the fence. There were three bottles still standing."

The sheriff glanced at Harris and continued, "Our boy looked at the bottles and I was looking at him. Suddenly, I heard something like WHOOMWHOOMWHOOM! All three bottles blew apart and there's Henry holding a smoking Peacemaker. Now maybe me and the crowd saw him move and maybe not. I think I got just a glimpse, a quick blur. Anyway, Harris turned to the agitator and said, 'I'd be grateful for anything you can show me.'"

Jack, Charlie, and Bubba all smiled at Henry's red face.

"And what did the young man do?" asked Murdock.

"He just stared at Harris," said Wilkie. "And it looked

like he'd shrunk a foot. Finally, he managed to say, 'I heard about you in Houston. I surely caint give you a lesson, but I got a suggestion to make.'

"Well everything started to loosen up when Henry smiled and asked, 'What's the suggestion?'

"You need to start selling tickets," said the stranger.

"So to end up," said Charlie, "the crowd slapped the young man on the back and took him to Kate's for a drink."

"And Harris gained a new insight about his reputation," said Murdock.

"Yep," said Wilkie. "Now he knew it stretched all the way to Houston."

"So then you took out after Whiteside," said Bubba.

Henry shrugged and said, "Yeah, I corralled Pat up in the Boot Heel and turned him over to the Carroll County sheriff. About a week later, I got back into Medford."

"In the meantime," said Wilkie, "I got news of another robbery. The Howe Lumber Company was operating a sawmill and finishing plant near the edge of Crowley's Ridge. Four men had held up their office and took off with the payroll. Again, it was an old bearded guy, accompanied by three younger men, but this time there was a positive identification by four witnesses. All four came into town and made out sworn statements."

"Pray tell us who the robbers were," murmured Murdock.

"Why no one else but our old friends Lucius, Seth, James and Bud. Seems this time the Jones gang hadn't even bothered to wear masks."

Harris said, "I got back into town as Charlie was rounding up a posse."

"It wasn't much of a posse," said Wilkie. "Just me, Dick, and a horse trader named Tyrell Banks. Henry agreed to go along, so that made four of us. Next morning we headed out and pointed ourselves toward the hills. After a couple of hours, our number got smaller. Dick made the mistake of talking about how crazy the Jones bunch was and Tyrell suddenly remembered he had some urgent business back in Medford. He took off and now it was three of us and four of them."

"I recall you saying they lived way back in the sticks," said Bubba

"Yeah, way up in the hills, where, as the saying goes, you have to *pipe in sunshine*. Oh, sorry Henry, I forgot that's where you're from."

Harris gave him a rueful grin as Wilkie continued, "Dick knew exactly where the cabin was. We figured to be into the hills by dark. We'd camp out overnight and reach the Jones place by mid-morning. Just before sundown we got a lucky break and was able to sleep under a roof. We happened across a deserted farm house, surrounded by what looked like thirty acres of cleared land. It lay in a valley on fairly level ground. Looked like rich ground, too."

Murdock raised his head and said, "Are you trying to drum up a sale, Charlie?"

The sheriff smiled at Harris and said, "Too late for that. What we were looking at turned out to be Henry's future farm. He checked out the deeds and took it over within the month."

"Well, I'll be damned," said Bubba.

"It was abandoned and I all I had to do was pay the back taxes," said Harris. "At the time, I didn't know what I was letting myself in for. Not much profit, but a whole lot of labor."

"It looks good now," ventured Bubba. "Henry's got a going concern out there."

"Well," said Wilkie, "it stopped your wandering and I didn't think anything could do that."

Murdock stretched and said, "Well, gentlemen, since it seems Charlie's tale is going to take up the rest of the day, I suggest we get a bite to eat."

"Now, that's a good idea, Jack," said Bubba. He still felt self-conscious using the first name. 'Mr. Murdock' would always seem more fitting.

The four men got up and walked out the door. Charlie locked it and they strolled down the plank sidewalk to Kate's Place. After the recent rain, the air smelled like newly washed linen. The sheriff took a deep breath. He looked up at a cobalt sky and squinted at the sun, now passed its meridian and blazing in the west. Half to himself, he murmured, "I wonder where they are now?"

"Wherever they are, they're getting close," said Bubba. "I can feel it."

"Yeah," said Wilkie. "I don't think they're wasting any time."

Harris said, "If that's so, they'll be east of Little Rock. Tonight should be their last sleep-out."

"One more day," said Bubba. He glanced around while an unbidden thought flashed through his brain. Will today be the last time I eat a supper or see a sunset or lay down in my bed? A chill ran through his body. He shook his head and stole a guilty look at his companions. There was his boss, walking beside him, looking dour as usual, but otherwise unworried. Behind them came Harris and Murdock, chatting about some saloon in Memphis. Bubba looked and listened and his apprehension faded.

The restaurant was about half full, echoing with the sounds of a dozen conversations. A narrow aperture stretched across the rear wall, separating kitchen from restaurant. Through it, they could see Marge tending an oven and instructing the help. Kate's assistant, Kerrie, stood behind the cash register. Nobody had ever ascertained exactly what job Kerrie held. She seemed to be all over the place, helping keep the hotel rooms clean, assisting Margie, or sometimes giving Dosh a hand behind the bar. A lot of her time was spent running errands for Kate Mulroney. Although pretty and friendly enough, she maintained a serious manner and tended to keep to herself. Harris learned from Katie that Kerrie lived with her mother on the outskirts of town. Bubba Dawkins was smitten with her.

Harris led the way to a corner table and they all sat down. Wilkie was amused to see that Henry and Jack immediately took the chairs with backs against the walls. Old habits certainly stuck with you. Kerrie came over with four menus and wrote down their orders. Everybody ordered the noon day special, a chicken and vegetable dinner.

Bubba's eyes never left Kerrie, and as she turned to go, he asked, "Will you be here during supper?"

The young girl gave him a slightly perplexed look. "I imagine I will, Bubba. We're a little short on help."

Bubba swallowed and allowed as how he hoped she would be, because he planned on being here, too. Kerrie revealed one of her infrequent smiles and walked back to the kitchen.

"Damn, Bubba," said the sheriff. "I sure wish I had your way with words. They'd sweep any woman off her feet." And in voice very much like his deputy's, he stammered, "Juh . . . Gee, Miss Kerrie, are you gonna be servin' supper here tonight. Uh, th...that's good, buh...because I'm gonna be eatin' here at the same time."

Harris and Murdock turned bemused smiles on Bubba, who blushed and responded, "Go ahead, sheriff. Have your fun."

Charlie winked at the other two and said, "Of course, he may be using the young girl to get to the mama."

Both men laughed, and Bubba, who understood no part of irony, said, "No, it's Kerrie. I know she ain't interested, but I can't help trying."

Black Jack smiled at the young deputy. "Don't be discouraged, Bubba. Perhaps fate will take a hand."

Bubba nodded and glanced at his boss. Charlie Wilkie had sure changed. Dawkins couldn't believe the sheriff was now teasing and joking instead of snarling and growling. It was definitely a change for the better, and Bubba, with his peculiar insight, thought he understood the reason. Men facing danger grow closer together.

Margie brought the food and placed it before them. "More coffee?" she asked. They nodded and she took a pot from the tray and filled their cups.

"Much obliged, ma'am," murmured Murdock.

Margie gave him a quick look. "You feeling a little more peaceable now?"

"Yes, indeed, ma'am. That is my natural state."

"Good to hear," said Margie. She smiled and added, "I don't like violence, but that carpetbagger was really begging for it."

"Have you seen him since then?" asked Murdock.

"Yep, he came downstairs right after you left and checked out. Kept looking over his shoulder. A few minutes later, he was in his buggy and headed out of town."

Murdock nodded and Wilkie asked, "Something I should know about?"

"Not at all," replied Black Jack. "Just a small contretemps between myself and a gentleman from the north. It's all settled now."

"Contretemps," snorted Margie, and headed to the kitchen.

Charlie shrugged and went back to his food.

The men finished eating, and after the dishes were cleared away, Charlie leaned back and filled his pipe.

"Well," said Murdock, "go on with your saga of the Joneses."

Wilkie grinned at him and continued: "Early next morning, we saddled up and headed deeper into the hills.

Dick Wessell led the way, and along about ten o'clock, we saw chimney smoke rising above the treetops. Dick pointed and said, 'That's the Jones place and I believe the boys are at home.' I was just a little surprised to find them there. They should have known this was the first place we'd look, and I said as much to Dick. Dick just grinned and said, 'Hell, Charlie, I told you they were crazy.' Well, as it turned out, they had another reason for being there, and we were about to find out what it was.

We came to the edge of a clearing and saw the Jones cabin, sitting in the middle of it and facing towards us. Off to one side, stood a ramshackle barn, and through the open entrance, we could see horses moving around. Harris, here, had the sharpest eyes and he noticed the horses were saddled. We decided to circle the clearing with the idea of approaching the cabin from behind. The woods were free of undergrowth, so we stayed on our mounts. Well, when we got half-way around, what we saw made us jerk the horses to a halt. There, at the rear of the cabin, were three men, standing side by side. Their backs were to us and they had their heads bowed.

I motioned to the others and we tied up our horses. Then we slipped a little closer. The men didn't move, but I knew they had to be our robbers. What I couldn't understand was what the hell they were doing. And where was the fourth Jones? All three were holding their hats, and while we watched, they straightened up, put their hats back on, and headed for the rear door of the cabin. What they left behind, and what was now visible to us, made everything clear. It was an oblong mound of loose dirt. The men had been standing over a fresh grave.

We eased back into the woods a bit and Dick said, 'Well, one of them is dead and I think I know which one.'

'Which one is it?' I whispered.

'It's the old man,' said Dick.

'How do you know?'

'The three we were looking at had brown hair, but the old man's hair is all over gray.'

'There wasn't any shooting at the saw mill,' I said. 'I wonder what happened to him?'

'I don't know,' said Dick, 'but we better move fast. Those horses are ready to be rode.'

Well, we palavered for a minute. Dick suggested we just storm the door and take them, but of course that could get one of us killed. Finally, an idea came to me and I said, 'Let's walk around to where the barn is.'

When we got there, it was just the way I'd hoped. There was no window on that side of the cabin. I told the others my plan and they both agreed. We sprinted from the woods and ducked into the barn. Dick climbed up to the loft and Henry and I concealed ourselves below. Everybody crouched in their positions, waiting for the brothers. We didn't have long to wait. Pretty soon, the cabin door slammed and we heard them coming toward the barn. I peeked through a crack in the wall and saw they were all packing pistols. The one they called Bud looked like he belonged in school, just a boy, but that hog leg on his hip brought him to adulthood in my eyes. They came in the doorway and walked straight to their horses. They never noticed Wessell, but I could see him, just above the loft ladder, looking down. His double-barreled shotgun was trained right on them. Henry and I raised up and stood behind them with our weapons drawn. We took a couple of steps forward and I said, 'Get you hands up, boys. We got guns on you.'

All three froze in place and two of them slowly raised their hands. But the boy, a mean little snake, whirled around and stood there with his right hand quivering over his holster.

I don't remember exactly what Harris told him, but it was something like, 'You're just a kid and I don't want to shoot you, but if them hands don't start going up, you ain't gonna get any older.' The youngster shot his hands up and all three stood there and cussed us like sailors. Seems their main gripe was that we were taking them away on the same day they'd buried their daddy, like they was supposed to get a jail holiday or something."

Harris said, "They kept it up all the way back to Medford. Didn't leave much doubt as to what they'd do to us if they ever got a chance."

"Yeah," said Wilkie. "And as I remember, even then, they brought Snake River Reese into it. He already had a reputation as a killer. They let us know he was their uncle and that he'd be taking a part."

"And as it turns out," murmured Harris, "they meant every word."

"I reckon they did," said the sheriff. "Anyway, all three went to trial and were found guilty of armed robbery. They sentenced them to ten years of hard labor at Tucker Prison."

"Even the boy?" queried Murdock

"Yeah, I kinda hated to see that," said Wilkie, "but, like I said, he was a mean little snake, and now he's probably meaner. You don't mellow much in prison and it ain't a place to mature. Bud will be a sixteen year old delinquent in a twenty-six year old body. When they come in, he'll be the one most likely to do something unpredictable."

Bubba turned to his boss. "You ever find out what killed the old man?"

"Nah," said Wilkie. "Probably his old black heart finally quit ticking."

Margie refilled their coffee cups. Harris took a sip and said, "What can you tell me about Robert Reese?"

He watched Wilkie and Murdock exchange glances, Wilkie nodding toward Jack.

Jack leaned closer and stated, "A killer, plain and simple. It's like a game to Mr. Reese and he's always trying to up the score." Harris caught the dark man's bleak smile. "And," Jack added, "he takes great pride in his skill."

"I imagine he has a right," said Harris

"Oh, I'm sure he does. Charlie and I have never actually seen the man in action, but according to all reports, he is blindingly fast and he does not miss. He is, of course, remorseless, and cannot be turned aside."

Henry didn't reply and he wasn't really thinking about the gunfighter. He was remembering something Jack had mentioned, and a stark picture formed in his mind. He saw it very clearly. There was a saloon in some forgotten town in east Kansas, and within it stood Black Jack Murdock, all alone and unafraid, bracing Robert Reese and calling him to account.

The four men finished their coffee and stood up from the table. John Murdock announced his intention of taking a nap, and perhaps later, playing a few hands of poker. Sheriff Wilkie returned to his office and Bubba continued on patrol.

Henry Harris walked over to the livery stable and checked on the gray. He gave the stable boy some instructions on how to mix the grain, then walked toward the outskirts of town and a nearby grove of trees. The lowering sun was caught in a nest of branches and a gentle wind carried the sound of buzzing insects and the faint aroma of wild mint. He found himself wishing Kate was here beside him, sharing this peaceful scene, and it took a moment to dismiss her from his mind.

Harris took a deep breath and swung his arms to loosen up the muscles. He strolled past the last building and turned toward the trees. A slender sycamore sapling reared up about twenty yards away. Henry stood facing it.

Back in his office, Wilkie heard the first report, which could only have come from a .44. Two more shots followed. He knew where they were coming from and who was doing the shooting. Sometimes he went to that same grove to practice. With a grim smile, the sheriff returned to his paperwork.

The young sapling was still quivering from the impact of the last bullet. The gun was back in its holster, but Harris didn't draw again. There was really no need. The previous performance had been beyond improvement, simple acts of lethal perfection that would have been, had the eye been able to follow them, quite beautiful to watch. A turtle dove sounded in the underbrush. Harris cocked an ear, but it did not call again. He slowly turned around and strolled back into town.

Chapter Five

John Murdock awoke from his nap, feeling refreshed. A fastidious man, he cleaned up as thoroughly as he could in the bedside wash basin and resolved to make use of the hotel tub tomorrow. Kate provided bathing facilities in a small room at the end of the hall. He came down the stairs and found Kate and Harris, bent over the counter talking to each other. They seemed engrossed in each other's words and Murdock hesitated, not wanting to interrupt.

Harris looked up and said, "Evening, Jack."

"Good evening, Henry. Evening, Miss Kate. Will you two join me in a bite of supper?"

Kate said, "I'm sure Henry will, but I'm afraid I have some paperwork to catch up on. Perhaps tomorrow night."

Both men looked at each other and Kate placed a hand over her mouth. "My God," she murmured.

"Don't worry, Miss Kate. It may be Saturday before we see any excitement."

"I suppose," she said, "but Henry tells me he expects them tomorrow night."

"Yes ma'am, and so do I."

Katie's voice came out high and strained. "Tomorrow night, Saturday, whichever it is, there's going to be a fight. And what will happen then, John?"

Jack's gaunt frame straightened and the black eyes burned. "They are evil men, Miss Kate, and they come to exact a shameful revenge. We will give them no quarter."

"Don't let them come on you by surprise."

Jack gave her a chilly smile. "Certainly not, ma'am. As a matter of fact, I think it is we who shall surprise them. They'll ride in expecting to confront a sheriff, grown older, and one lone deputy. Instead they will meet a somewhat different assortment."

"Indeed they will," she said, looking from one to the other, but she retained a worried frown. "I was also thinking about innocent bystanders." And with a quick twitch of the lips added, "I wouldn't want to lose any customers."

In a gentler tone, Murdock answered, "We'll try to be mindful of them. And Mr. Harris and myself will look forward to dining with you tomorrow night."

Kate nodded and turned to Harris. "I'll see you when I've finished."

He touched her on the shoulder and she smiled and walked away. Murdock watched this exchange, sensing a depth of devotion.

Jack followed Harris into the restaurant. Their corner table was occupied by three dusty travelers, so he pointed to a place by the window. Harris nodded and they seated themselves so as to have a clear view of their surroundings. Murdock glanced at the corner table and gave Harris a questioning look.

Henry inspected the three men and shook his head. "Thanks for trying to put Katie at ease," he said.

"I was simply telling the truth, Harris." Murdock's face grew grim again and the statement came out flat and factual. "Before much more time has passed, Snake River Reese will lie stinking in the ground, along with all the Jones boys."

A waitress, young and smiling, brought over coffee and took their order. Henry asked for the steak dinner and Jack, looking down the menu, decided on scrambled eggs and a biscuit. When the food came, Henry looked at Murdock's plate and quipped, "Eat hearty."

"When I was younger, I was indeed a hearty eater, but after a couple of years of war, that was no longer possible. Rations grew progressively scarce, and at the end, there was no food at all. My stomach shrunk to the size of a turnip and I do not believe it has enlarged much since."

"You were with General Lee on the very last day."

"To the very last hour, sir, along with all his gallant soldiers."

"I would very much liked to have met him."

Black Jack pushed his half-finished dinner aside and gazed thoughtfully out the window. And what he saw past the glass was never any part of Medford. "You would not have forgotten the meeting," he said. "And, I daresay, you would have remembered the man instead of the general. That speaks volumes for the man, because the general was admired and respected by an entire country, both north and south. As a man, he was always kind, gentle, and considerate, and he was also a very simple soul. That's what his enemies and even his compatriots never understood, his innate and utter simplicity." Murdock sighed and turned from the window. "On that last day, we were at Appomattox Court House, and when the final hour came, Robert E. Lee rode up to the McLean home, accompanied by his aide, Colonel Marshall. The men knew what was up and they begged him not to go, begged him to let them fight, just one more day. These were soldiers without food, without ammunition or any other supplies, and basically without hope. Yet they wanted to continue the fight. Not from pride or love of country, but simply for their general."

"Well John," said Harris. "It's all over now."

"Yes it is, my friend. The Lost Cause. That's what people are calling it. Well, maybe it should have been lost. To be honest, I was never comfortable with slavery. We benefited from it, but many of us believed it to be wrong. Kate Mulroney's father refused to employ it, thus showing more character than I and the other planters. Also, we were fighting a new age, the Industrial Age, which, I'm afraid, was destined to prevail."

"But if you and I had it to do over again, what do you think we'd do?"

"The same thing, of course," laughed Murdock. "Our state would again take precedence, along with our family and neighbors. As Mississippi and Arkansas went, so we would go. There was never really any option."

Harris nodded and continued with his steak.

Murdock rose and said, "If' you'll excuse me, I believe I'll take a few hands at yon poker table. Will you join me when you finish devouring that hunk of beef?"

Henry smiled and said, "Not tonight. I promised the sheriff I'd help Bubba make his rounds. Charlie's not so young anymore. He needs to get some sleep."

"Better not let Charlie hear you say that. Do you need any help?"

"No, and I probably won't be out for long. When things quiet down, I'll turn in, too. By the way, I think Charlie wants to see us tomorrow morning.'

"Murdock plucked his hat from the table and said, "No doubt he has some plans to lay out."

"Probably," murmured Harris, past a mouthful of meat.

"I'll be there," said Murdock.

Kerrie was at the cash register and Murdock paid for himself and Harris's meals.

"Was everything all right?" she asked.

"Very good, ma'am. And how are you this evening?"

"Fine, thank you, Mr. Murdock." She deposited the money, and looking up, was surprised to see the spare figure still standing in front of her.

"Miss Kerrie," said Murdock, "I do not usually interest myself in the personal affairs of others, but I feel there's something you should know."

"Yes?"

"Young Bubba Dawkins is quite taken with you. I do not know if you are aware of this. Possibly you are, and his feelings are unrequited. In any case, I felt I should mention it."

Kerrie grinned. "And why is that, Mr. Murdock?"

"I've grown fond of the lad and will have to depend on him in a coming crisis. I don't believe he'll let me down."

"Thank you for bringing it to my attention," said the young woman, and matching his formality as so many did, added, "I don't feel the situation is entirely hopeless."

Jack smiled and gave a short bow. "May I say that Bubba's discernment is of the first order." He headed through the door and turned toward the saloon.

Henry watched Jack walk out, a lean figure in dark clothing, the pipe stem legs jack-knifing back and forth. He wondered what the conversation with Kerrie had been about. The steak tasted good. He chewed on the last morsel and stared out the window. The street had darkened, and here and there, some hanging lanterns cast a yellow glow. A few evening strollers passed by the window and one or two waved at the figure inside. Henry felt suddenly exposed. He got up and walked over to Kerrie.

"John Murdock paid for both meals," she said.

"Guess I owe him one."

"How was the steak?"

"Real good, Kerrie. Nice and tender."

"Is Bubba working tonight?"

"Yeah, as a matter of fact, I'm gonna help him for awhile."

"Well, when you see him, tell him about the steak."

Harris looked at her and blinked. "Why sure, Kerrie. He'll probably be in later."

"That'll be nice," she murmured.

Henry walked out into the street and looked left and right. Would they come in tonight, he wondered. Was it possible? He stood for a moment, then dismissed the thought. Not possible, but he wouldn't be able to say the same thing tomorrow. In the distance, he spied Dawkins checking the door on Sammie's Boutique. Harris walked up to him. "The sheriff is turning in early tonight. I told him I'd give you some help, that is if you want it."

"Why sure. If it ain't too much trouble. I usually walk the streets about this time."

"Lead the way," said Harris.

Dawkins glanced once more at the dress shop and gave a soft chuckle.

"What's the joke, Bubba?"

So Bubba related the story of Charles Wilkie, Donald Lacey, and Sammie Davis's brassier. Henry burst out laughing and so did Bubba. The laughter felt good, and with it came a lifting of the deputy's anxiety. He reflected that in any kind of danger, he would not have swapped his three companions for any other men on earth.

"Well," said Henry, "if you're looking for a coward, don't go around the sheriff's office."

"Well told," said Bubba. And then, without thinking, he added, "I hope that includes his deputy."

Henry looked at Bubba and resisted an impulse to place his hand on the young man's shoulder. "It does, Bubba," he said, "and none of us have ever thought otherwise."

They finished the early evening patrol and Harris asked the deputy if he felt like eating.

"Sure do," Bubba replied.

"Well, I've already finished my supper, so you go ahead."

Bubba started off and Harris said, "Oh by the way, Kerrie asked about you. Wanted to know if you were coming by. Said the steak was real good tonight."

Bubba's blush went unseen in the darkness. He murmured, "Aw come on, Henry. The sheriff ain't enough. I got to get it from you, too?"

Harris gave Dawkins a sober look. "I never tease a man about a woman, Bubba. It's bad business, and it could be dangerous."

"You mean Kerrie really said that?"

At that moment, the deputy looked so like a young boy, Henry Harris felt as ancient as dirt. "You bet she did."

Dawkins grinned and hurried away. Harris walked to the end of the street, turned back, and stopped at the sheriff's office. Wilkie had gone home, but this time he'd left the door unlocked. Harris lifted the latch and walked inside. He strolled back to the room, containing the three jail cells. Two were empty but the third held a field hand, arrested for drunk and disorderly. The man raised up in his cot and blinked at Henry.

Harris stopped and stared at the prisoner. "How's it going, Oscar?"

Oscar Pinnegar rubbed his eyes and said, "That you, Harris? What the hell are you doin' wearing a badge?"

Harris figured this was the only man in town who didn't know about the Jones boys. "Oh, just helping Wilkie out for a couple of days. Have you had your supper?"

"Yeah, one of Kate's gals brought it over."

"How long you in for?"

"Two weeks. Caint make bail, so I'll reckon I'll spend the full time."

"What did you do?"

"Got drunk and threw a chair across Dosh's bar."

"For that you got two weeks? That sounds a little harsh."

Oscar dropped his head and gave Harris a sheepish look. "Well, maybe not. At the time, that chair had a traveling salesman in it."

Harris gave a chuckle, shook his head, and walked back out the door. He reached the sidewalk again and headed down one of the side streets. Charles Wilkie's house stood on the left, but Henry decided not to stop. He figured Charlie's wife wouldn't appreciate it. She, like everyone else, knew what was coming and must want some time with her husband. They'd been married many years and Henry reflected that Annie was the only person alive who could face down Charlie Wilkie. It also crossed his mind that concern for a wife was one distraction he'd never had to worry about, and at this particular moment, he was glad that this was so.

Roses grew in the couple's front yard and the air was full of their fragrance. Henry took a deep breath, savoring the scent before moving on down the street. Finally, he headed back uptown. A little later Dawkins returned with a smile pasted on his face. Neither man mentioned Katie's assistant.

Gradually the night quieted down and most of the lights blinked out. Only Kate's Place remained alive and humming, the windows all aglow.

"Harris turned to his partner and said, "Well, I guess I'll call it a night."

"Okay," said Bubba. "Listen, I appreciate you helping me for awhile. And for letting me get some supper."

"I take it the meal was pleasant."

Bubba grinned and gave him a sideways look. "Real pleasant."

"When are you going to knock off?"

"Sheriff Wilkie likes for me to patrol until nine o'clock. Then, I stay at the office for a couple of hours. After that, it's bed time."

"Until something happens," said Harris.

"Yeah, it hardly ever does, but if there's trouble, they wake me up. If it's serious enough, I wake up Charlie."

"Okay, Bubba. Try to get some rest tonight."

"Cause I'm gonna need it, right?"

"Very probably," answered Harris.

"Did Charlie tell you about the meeting tomorrow?"

"Yep, see you then."

Harris turned away and walked toward Kate's. He glanced over his shoulder and saw Bubba Dawkins staring after him. Man oh man, he thought, what must the boy be going through. Hell, if I was him instead of me, I'd be in Texas by now."

Charlie Wilkie sat at the kitchen table, drinking a final cup of coffee. He felt fatigue settling over him like a heavy blanket. He let his eyelids close, for a moment, and came near to dozing. He came back to with a start and saw Annie staring at him. He'd watched that gentle face for thirty years, observed its many expressions, and had come to read them all. Now he saw a naked concern. He also saw the same beauty that had been hers as a bride, coming down the aisle. He tried to summon up some reassuring words, but drew a great big blank.

She smiled at him and said, "It's getting late. Time for old folks to be in bed."

He lifted his cup and said, "Soon as I finish this. You go ahead, baby."

"No, I'll wait for you."

"I guess Bubba is doing okay."

"Yes, I saw him out the window about an hour ago. I also saw Henry Harris."

"Yeah, Henry's helping out tonight. Hell, he's deputized. So is Murdock. They should be earning their pay."

"They'll earn it later," she said. Charlie gave her a sharp look, but she continued, "You know, I've never meddled in your work."

In his old gruff tone he answered, "But you're gonna meddle now."

"Yes, I intend to meddle now."

"Mind telling me why?"

"Charles Wilkie, you know why. This is something different. Something very dangerous. I'm not a fool. I understand what's coming."

"Well hell. I've been in tough scrapes before."

"Yes, and I was there, too. Those scrapes don't measure up to this." She leaned over and said, "And because I love you, I can say this, Charlie. You're not as young as you used to be."

Wilkie's face clouded over and he felt his temper rise. Then it subsided and he gave out a sigh. He could seldom be angry with Annie. "Just what sort of meddling did you have in mind?"

"I want to know some things. I want to know what's on your side. What's on *our* side."

"Three good men are on our side."

"You used to have some reservations about Bubba."

Wilkie wouldn't lie to her. It was time to be earnest with the only person who'd ever really mattered. He leaned forward and said, "I've still got some reservations, but he's coming along. I don't believe he'll fail us."

"But is he skillful enough?"

Annie could always cut to the heart of the matter. He gave her an approving glance. "Not as skillful as the other two, but he'll know what to do when the time comes, and he won't shirk his duty."

"Harris is very good, isn't he?"

Now it was easy to be earnest. "He's more than that, Annie. He's a wizard at what he does. I've never seen the like."

"And Black Jack Murdock?"

"John Murdock is a force, and fear don't enter into his makeup. I imagine Black Jack will unnerve that bunch even more than Henry Harris."

"I only know him as a kind and considerate gentleman."

"Well, I reckon he's that, too."

"Very well," said Annie. "I'm through meddling, except for a final statement."

"Go ahead," said Charlie.

"I think my husband's enemies should also go in fear of him."

Charlie gave his wife a tight hug. "Let us go to bed, my dear. And I'll demonstrate to you that my youth hasn't entirely fled."

"What about your coffee?" She grinned.

The sheriff walked to the sink and slowly turned the cup over.

Annie blew out the lamp, and arm in arm, they headed up the stairs.

* * *

Bubba had almost finished his last patrol for the night. He stopped to peer up and down the deserted street, enjoying the peaceful silence, when all at once he felt a brief prescience of blazing guns and fallen men. For a second, it was all terribly real and then it faded away and Bubba put it from his mind. He stood opposite Kate's Place trying to decide whether to check out the saloon or return to the office. He really wanted to sit down for awhile, but decided the saloon needed checking. Besides, he might run into Kerrie. He hoisted his holster, and for a moment, his hand played over the butt of the old Colt Dragoon. Its weight felt reassuring.

Bubba crossed the street and stood before the hotel entrance. He knocked the dust from his clothing, adjusted his hat, and stepped inside. The restaurant had closed and the lobby was empty of people. Bubba's heart lightened when he saw Kerrie standing behind the counter, looking like all the pretty girls in all his dreams, looking like all his hopes come true. She was busy making entries in a leather bound ledger. As Bubba approached the counter, she looked up, smiled, and laid the ledger aside.

"I thought you had finished your rounds," she said.

"I have, just about. I'm gonna check the saloon, then stay at the jail for a couple of hours. After that, I'll be through for the night."

"I'll be finishing up about the same time."

Bubba throat tightened. He wondered it she was hinting she'd like to see him. Could it be? He wasn't sure. He started to respond, but his courage failed him. Instead he muttered, "Well, I guess I'd better check on Dosh."

He was almost to the swinging doors, when he heard her voice behind him. "Bubba Dawkins, are you going to walk me home or not?"

He turned quickly and said, "Why sure, Kerrie. I was gonna ask you, but I—"

"I'll be waiting at eleven o'clock," she said.

Bubba blushed right on cue. "I can't wait for it to get here."

Kerrie returned to her ledger and murmured, "That's better, Mr. Dawkins."

Bubba pushed through the doors and stopped just inside. He was greeted by the usual noise: a tinny piano, so out of tune it always made him smile, the hoots and laughter of half drunk patrons, and the clink of bottles and glasses. Through layers of tobacco smoke, he could make out the long bar with Dosh Colson behind it. Old Dosh was hopping from one end to the other, filling glasses, uncapping bottles of beer, and talking to the barflies.

He caught sight of Dawkins and called, "Look who's here. How's it going, Bubba?"

"Looks like you got a crowd."

"Not bad for a Thursday night. Matter of fact, it's damn good, but it'll thin out before long, starting to get late." He walked to the end of the bar and waited for Bubba to join him.

"Heard any more news?" he asked.

"Not a word," said Bubba. "But we know they're coming."

"When you figure they'll get here?"

"Tomorrow afternoon. Tomorrow night. Maybe Saturday."

"I expect 'em late tomorrow," said Dosh. "They ain't gonna get side-tracked."

Bubba felt a tug on his shirt sleeve, and looked around to see who had joined them. Sam Hyzer's wizened, wrinkled face was turned upward toward him. Sam had long been the town's only barber and the main source of all town gossip.

The little man tilted his hat over one eye and declared. "Okay, gents. Very good. We all know they'll be here in short order. Question is, whaddaya gonna do to protect the citizens of this town. What's to keep 'em from just shootin' anybody they please, once they get here."

"Look Sam," answered Dawkins. "They won't be coming just to start shooting people at random. They've made definite plans, and we're making plans to deal with them. Now, when you open up that barber shop tomorrow, just tell everybody that Friday night could bring some trouble. Toward dark, they should all hurry home and stay there till the trouble is over."

Hyzer hitched up his pants and straightened his hat. "Fine deputy, but I just hope for your sake, and for our sakes, that those plans of yours are good ones." Nodding once at Dosh, he turned and headed toward the swinging doors.

Dawkins looked out over the floor. A few men had gathered behind the piano player, while a half dozen others leaned against the walls. All the tables were full. Three smaller tables, reserved for poker, sat in a far corner and these were also occupied. John Murdock sat at one of them, a thin cigar in his mouth, the deep-set eyes fixed on his cards. Murdock's hat hung on the near wall. His long raven hair and the black broadcloth presented an image of darkness and he seemed to soak in the lamp light. Bubba wondered if that was why they called him Black Jack. Not on account of his deeds, but simply because of the way he looked. Jack spotted the deputy and nodded.

Bubba turned to Dosh and said, "Yessir, sure is a mess of people. It's like a Saturday night. I haven't seen some of these folks for months."

"And it'll be months before you see 'em again." The bartender peered at Dawkins. "They're here to see the gunfight, Bubba."

"What?"

"Uh-huh. I've overheard some talk. You can bet there'll be a lot more folks tomorrow."

"Well, I'll be damned. I don't suppose any of them would care to be deputized."

Dosh polished a spot on the bar and gave a humorless chuckle, "No, and I don't blame 'em. I guess you heard that I was asked."

"Yeah, I heard, but hell Dosh, you've taken your share of risks. Besides, you got a family now."

Colson nodded and headed back down the bar. Dawkins strolled over to Murdock's table. Besides Jack, there were two other players, plus the house dealer. Bubba said, "Evening, Jack."

"Why, good evening, deputy. You're keeping late hours tonight."

"So are you," said Bubba. And eyeing the pile of chips in front of Murdock, he added, "but I imagine you'll make more money than I will."

"That is entirely possible. The cards have not been kind to these two gentlemen."

"Kindness ain't got nothing to do with it," growled one of the players.

Bubba glanced over at the speaker, a sour-faced, rough looking man he'd never seen before.

The man glared at Murdock and said, "Well, come on Mister. You gonna stay and play or keep talkin' to the lawdog here?"

Murdock shrugged and pitched in five dollars. The man to his left also anted up.

Bubba looked down at Murdock and murmured, "A five dollar ante? That's pretty rich. What's the bet limit?"

Murdock said. "The gentleman with the limited supply

of patience has insisted we be allowed to go as high as fifty dollars."

"Whew," breathed Bubba.

"I got all the patience I need," exclaimed the loud mouth, "and I don't claim to be no gentleman. Fact of the business is, I don't appreciate bein' called one."

"Then how shall I address you, sir?" Murdock's voice, Bubba noticed, held a faint trace of amusement. Otherwise, he might have been talking to someone about the price of oats.

The man didn't answer and the player on Murdock's left said, "His name's Lacey." Lacey scowled at the player, but remained silent.

Bubba pricked up his ears, remembering Donald Lacey and the Butterfly Saloon.

The player stared back at Lacey and asked, "Can you open?"

Lacey studied his cards and murmured, "I'll open for ten."

Everybody stayed. Bubba glanced down at Jack's hand and saw he was holding three queens.

The dealer looked at Lacey and said, "How many you need, pardner?"

Lacey threw down three cards and said, "Gimme three." He looked at the cards dealt him and his lips twitched in a smile. Murdock was watching him.

Jack's turn came and he said. "I'll take two."

Bubba again looked at Murdock's cards. The dealer had given him a queen and a nine. Now he was holding four of a kind. The final player drew three cards.

Lacey glanced at his hand, and without hesitation, said, "Bet thirty dollars."

"Damn," said the other player, "you out for the quick kill?"

"I would've bet fifty, but I didn't want to scare you off," laughed Lacey.

"Well you might have anyway, but we'll see."

Murdock considered the loud mouth, sighed, and said, "I'll call and raise you twenty."

The other player called but his hand trembled as he tossed in fifty dollars worth of chips.

All eyes were on Lacey, who shoved two of his ten dollar chips forward and said, "I'll call." Then, he tossed in five more and shouted, "And I'll raise you fifty."

Things got quiet at the surrounding tables and a few customers wandered over to watch. The man playing with Lacey and Murdock turned his cards over and said, "Fold."

Lacey hunched over the table and fixed Murdock in a stare of pure malice. "Well, Mr. Fancy Man. What do you say to that?"

Black Jack gazed at his hand with a slightly bored expression. He tapped his cards with a thin forefinger and looked up at Lacey. "Well sir, the first thing I say is that I dislike being called a 'Fancy Man' about as much as you dislike being called a gentleman. The first does not describe me and the latter definitely does not apply to you. Secondly, I say that your fifty dollar bet is called."

Lacey flushed and his eyes darted about the room. For the first time, he looked uncertain, as if he'd been taken to a place he did not care to be. A second look at his cards restored his composure. He lay them face up on the table, and in a triumphant tone announced, "Four sixes." He reached for the pile of chips and, grinning at the dealer, said, "I started with two and drawed two more. I'm one lucky bastard tonight."

Murdock's soft voice came from across the table. "I'm afraid, sir, that only half of your statement is true. The game of poker has changed slightly over the years, but four ladies will always beat the same number of sixes."

A few of the onlookers gasped and Lacey stared, transfixed and bug-eyed, at the four queens spread before him.

Then, he gave a strangled cry and lunged across the table toward Murdock. Black Jack rose and drew in one smooth motion, and suddenly the gambler was peering at the barrel of a very large gun, the bore looking big as a cannon. Bubba walked over and plucked a pistol from the gambler's belt. Remembering Lacey's remark, he said, "You know, it's a felony crime to attack a lawdog."

Lacey straightened up and said, "I never attacked you."

Dawkins looked at Murdock and said, "Jack?"

Murdock reached down and slowly pulled his coat back. Pinned to his shirt was a shiny, bronze badge. Lacey gaped at it and then at the one on Bubba's chest. "Y'all are in this together," he yelled. "You probably got the game rigged."

Murdock holstered his gun and walked around to where Lacey stood. Leaning close, he murmured, "Mr. Lacey, please try not to speak. Any further words will, I assure you, be dangerous to your health."

Lacey was held in the dark man's gaze. Murdock nodded to Bubba and said, "I believe the other deputy wishes to talk to you."

"Are you related to Donald Lacey?" asked Bubba.

The trouble maker was still staring at Murdock.

"You may speak now," said Jack.

"He's my cousin," answered Lacey.

"He's also in prison for robbery. I understand dress shops are his specialty."

Lacey's face grew red. "That's what that lyin' sheriff said. He framed Donald, but now he's gonna pay. Just wait till the Jones boys finish with him."

"Is that why you're in town," asked Dawkins, "to see it happen?"

"Damn right," said Lacey.

Murdock walked back to his chair and sat down. "Too

bad you won't be able to," he said. "There's no windows in our jail cells."

Bubba ushered Lacy toward the exit. Before going out the swinging doors, he looked back at the table. Another player had sat down and the dealer was flipping out cards as if nothing had happened. The game was back in progress. The two men marched passed Kerrie, who peered at the stranger.

"Everything okay?" she asked.

"Sure," said Bubba. "I'll see you at eleven."

Dawkins took his prisoner to the jail and locked him in the cell next to Oscar Pinnegar. Oscar raised his head from the cot and said, "Hey Bubba, can I get a drink of water?"

"Sure thing," said Dawkins. "I'll get you some."

While Bubba was in the next room, Lacey walked to the bars dividing the cells and Bubba heard him ask, "What's that deputy's last name?"

"Dawkins," said Oscar.

"How long's he been a deputy?"

"Oh, I dunno, less than a year, I think. Why?"

"No reason," said Lacey, and Dawkins heard him walk back to his bunk.

Bubba brought Oscar a dipper of water and was about to go when Lacey called out to him.

He paused and said, "What now, Lacey?"

"I know what you did to my cousin, Donald."

"So?"

"So, you shouldn't have took this job, deputy. You're gonna die with your sheriff. I may not get to see it, but I'll be there to piss on your graves."

Dawkins couldn't resist. He walked back to the cell, peered through the bars, and said, "Listen, you ignorant son of a bitch. That big mouth of yours came close to getting you killed tonight and you're too stupid to know it." He leaned closer. "That other deputy scared you, didn't he? Well, don't feel too bad. Black Jack Murdock has scared better men than you. When he gets that Black Jack look on him, why, even Henry Harris might get nervous."

Lacey sank back on his cot. "What's the gunfighter got to do with it?"

"Oh, didn't I mention it? Mr. Harris has decided to help us, too. He's our third deputy."

As Bubba went through the door he heard Oscar Pinnegar slap his knee and cackle. Back at Wilkie's desk, he poured a cup of water and took it to Oscar. He came back out, sat at the sheriff's desk, and recalled his actions in the saloon. Well, he thought, I handled Lacey all right, that is, with Murdock's help. But what about tomorrow? Then the words of Wilkie and Wessell floated through his mind. "You must never, ever back down," and, "When the killing time comes, you must not hesitate." Bubba hoped these words would serve him well.

He glanced at his pocket watch and saw it was close to eleven o'clock. Kerrie was waiting when he got to Kate's Place. She placed a shawl around her shoulders and they walked out together. Her street was unlit, but a crescent moon shone from the cloudless sky and helped to guide their steps.

Kerrie took his arm and said, "I'm glad we finally got around to this."

"Me too," answered Bubba. He was silent for a bit, then said, "I reckon I just didn't have the backbone to up and ask you."

"You're shy, Bubba. I am, too, but I figured if I didn't say something, we'd never take this walk."

"Well, I'm glad you did."

"Anyway, backbone has nothing to do with it. If you were a coward, you wouldn't be backing the sheriff."

Bubba halted, for a moment, and said, "I'd be lyin' if I told you I wasn't scared."

The young woman searched his face and softly said, "Bubba, being scared and being a coward are not the same things."

"I reckon," he murmured.

They continued on to her house and paused by the front gate. "Can I count on us doing this again?" she asked.

"You sure can Kerrie, but probably not for the next couple of nights."

"I know," she answered, "but just in case, tomorrow night, I get off at seven."

"I'll remember."

Suddenly, she leaned forward and kissed him on the mouth. "Be very careful," she whispered, and went in through the gate.

Bubba walked back to Sadie's Boarding House and climbed the stairs to his room. He stripped off his clothes and lay down on the narrow bed. For the first time in three nights, he lay there without worrying about the Jones bunch. Instead, he thought only of how Kerrie's lips felt, pressed against his own.

John Murdock reached for his hat and said, "That's it for me, boys."

One of the players said, "You mean to say you're gonna quit winners?"

There was no malice in it. Murdock smiled and said, "Gentlemen, if any of you can explain how it's better to quit losers, I may stay for awhile."

The other three laughed and Murdock walked to the bar. Dosh Colson was still serving drinks, but the passing hours had taken the spring out of his step. He turned a weary eye on Murdock and said, "What'll you have?"

"A whiskey, please."

Colson poured a shot glass full and Murdock tossed it back. He motioned for another and Dosh refilled the glass. The bartender held out his hand and said, "I'm Dosh Colson."

Murdock took the hand and shook it once. "Pleased to meet you, sir. My name is Murdock."

"Yes, I know. Black Jack Murdock."

Murdock stared at him and Colson added, "Charlie told me about you."

"I see."

"Bit of trouble at the table tonight?"

"Nothing to speak of. The gentleman placed too high a value on four sixes."

"I saw the badge," said Colson. "It's good to know you're helping Charlie."

"Well, the sheriff has come to my aid on a few occasions. Just returning the favor."

"Charlie's a good man."

"He is indeed." Murdock downed the second drink. "Well, goodnight, Mr. Colson."

"Goodnight, Mr. Murdock."

Colson watched the lean figure go out the swinging doors. A elderly man, wearing denim overalls, lifted a hand and said, "Gimme another beer, Dosh." Colson brought the beer and the man said, "Was that really Jack Murdock?"

"Sure was."

"Hot damn. I'm starting to feel sorry for them Jones boys."

Colson eyed the customer and said, "Well Jimmy, I wouldn't get all teary eyed just yet. There's lots that can happen, and most of it will probably be unexpected."

"Well, I don't intend to miss it," said Jimmy. "How about you?"

Colson wiped at an imaginary spot on the bar. "I already have, Jimmy. I already have."

Murdock paused at the hotel counter. One of Kate's helpers stood behind it. "Have you seen Miss Kerrie?" he asked. The girl gave him a bold look and replied, "She's gone for the night. I believe the deputy took her home."

Murdock smiled and continued up the stairs. Behind him, he heard the girl murmur, "Tall, dark, and handsome."

His room was unlit but Jack didn't bother with the lamp. He slowly removed his clothing and lay across the bed. Staring up at an unseen ceiling, he placed a bony hand across his stomach and gave a small sigh. His tender insides were rebelling against the two whiskeys. I should have drunk some milk, he thought. He breathed deeply and tried to clear his mind, but indefinite memories hovered just beyond his comprehension. Then they coalesced and flew backward and he found himself thinking of Eleanor, his long dead wife. She lay buried on what was once their plantation. When this was over, he planned to visit her grave. Before the war, she had been his companion, his confidant, and his constant love. In the darkness, it was not necessary to close his eyes in order to summon up the visions. Eleanor, running down the steps to greet him, yellow hair streaming behind her. Eleanor beside him, riding over their fields, gracefully sitting atop her mare, Little Lucy. And Eleanor, reaching for him in the night.

When news of her death came to him in the Shenandoah, the grief almost killed him. And when his leave was refused, he came very close to desertion. Two things kept him to his duty. The needs of his men and the sure knowledge that Eleanor would not have approved. Her image hovered above Jack Murdock's bed, and slightly comforted, he drifted into a dreamless sleep.

* * *

Henry Harris lay on his bed with both eyes closed. The door to his room swung back and he smelled the familiar lavender. Katie stood framed in the opening, back lit by the hallway light, and wearing a velvet robe. He wondered if she wore anything beneath it. She held a lamp level with her face and its light fled into the darkness of her hair and eyes. Once, Henry had mentioned her coloring, saying, "I thought the Irish were all blue-eyed and red-headed."

"Some, but not all," she'd replied. "Have ye not heard of th' Black Irish, my love?"

It amused him that she could so easily slip into the dialect. "Are they different in any way except appearance?"

"Oh, yes," she'd replied. "The lighter Irish are carefree and have a love of music and whiskey. The dark ones are of a thoughtful turn, and also very earnest. They seldom forget a kindness and never forget an injury. They are not long on forgiveness."

"Guess I'd better be careful, then."

"See that ye are," she'd replied.

Now, Kate sat on his bed and whispered, "Are you asleep?"

Henry produced a loud, stage snore and she swatted his face with her fingers. He laughed and pulled her to him.

She held the lamp away and cried, "Henry Harris, do you want to set fire to the bed?"

"Yes," he replied, "but not with that lamp."

Kate disentangled herself and sat back up. "Let's go down to my quarters. I'll go first and you follow."

Henry said, "Katie, I think we're long past fooling anybody."

"Probably so, but I still like to keep up appearances."

She left the room and Henry dressed quickly. Buckling his gun belt on, he went down the stairs and made a sharp turn to the right. Katie's door was just beside the stairwell. He rapped lightly, opened the door, and stepped inside.

The room was softly lit by shaded lamps and he smelled the familiar scent of lilac and furniture polish. He remembered the massive oak table, still sitting on the left, that Katie used for a desk. Its surface was littered with ledgers and papers. A couch and two padded chairs sat in front of him, and on his right, stood Katie's piano. Its dark surface glimmered in the lamp glow. A rear door opened and Katie came out of the bedroom wearing a green silk night gown. Henry looked past her at the huge, four-poster bed. Katie left the door open and came into his arms.

"Would you like a drink?" she asked.

"Sure."

She walked to a cabinet behind the oak table and brought forth a bottle and two glasses. The bottle was the twin of the one Dosh Colson kept behind his bar. Kate led him to the couch and they sat and sipped their drinks.

Henry looked around and said, "I see you've made some changes."

"Not a lot. Just the wallpaper. And I hung a couple of portraits."

"You didn't like the old wallpaper?"

"I just got tired of it. Besides, it was plain." Glancing at the walls, she added, "Now I've got a rose pattern."

Harris smiled and gave her a fond look. "You know, Katherine Mulroney, I've never told you this, but I'm proud of you. You've done well in this town."

"Well, I admit to having worked hard. That's mostly what counts."

"Having a head on your shoulders counts, too."

Katie looked at him and said, "And having you on my side."

Harris reddened and looked away. "I always have been," he murmured.

Katie laughed and said, "I remember you used to come through town with your wild ways. I was a little afraid of you then. Everybody was."

"Well, I was sort of rootless. You know, just drifting along."

"Yes, I know. But then you settled on that farm and a big change came over you. I know how much that place means to you. Yet once you mortgaged it to help me add my saloon." She placed a hand on his arm. "I remember you rounded up Charlie and a couple of city councilman and took them to the bank. I never knew what happened, but the money they loaned me was a lot more than your farm was worth."

"You paid them back with interest," he said.

"Of course, but I've never forgotten that. And another thing. You think I don't know why Kate's Place has never suffered any serious violence or trouble? It's because the rowdies know Henry Harris would take a personal interest."

"Well, it's sure personal," replied Harris.

"When did it get that way, I wonder."

He studied the dark-haired woman. "What brought all *this* on?"

Katie sat her glass on a low coffee table and turned toward him. On her face was that expression Henry had come to think of as her Irish...*Black Irish?* look. "You know damn well what's bringing this on, why I'm talking like this. By this time tomorrow, the Jones brothers will be in town, along with their black-hearted uncle. And you, hell all of you, except maybe Bubba, are sashaying around like everything's hunky dory."

Henry chuckled and placed a hand on her knee. "Relax Kate. We know what we're up against. And," he added softly, "they don't."

"If you say so," she muttered, and downed her glass of scotch.

"Besides, if it'll make you feel any better, I think Murdock is starting to get jittery."

Kate laughed in spite of herself. "He doesn't figure into it. That man's got ice water for blood. Everybody knows that."

Henry got up and walked over to the piano. "Well, Kate Mulroney, why don't you play me a tune. It's been awhile since I heard one."

Kate sighed, came over, and sat before the piano. "Kathleen Mavourneen?"

Harris nodded and the notes to the old Irish ballad floated softly across the room.

Kathleen Mavourneen, the gray dawn is breaking
The horn of the hunter is heard on the hill.

Kathleen's lover is going off to war. He has come to say goodbye, but she remains in bed. He patiently waits outside her window, before finally turning away.

It may be for years, and it and it may be forever,
But Kathleen Mavourneen is slumbering still.

Henry's hand rested lightly on her shoulder. Kate finished playing and sat silent before the piano. Henry gently stroked her cheek. Neither said a word.

...It may be forever...

Finally she arose and came into his arms. They held each other close. Then Kate, still without speaking, led him into her bedroom and closed the door behind them.

Chapter Six

Friday

Bud Jones lay on his hard, narrow cot, which was anchored to the rear wall above the one other cot in his cell. He'd awakened a moment ago and the first thing he noticed, as always, was the smell, a disgusting combination of stale sweat and foul mattresses and unclean air. And since the slop buckets had not been emptied of their nightly deposits, there came also the nostril numbing reek of crap and urine. He took shallow breaths until the stench became bearable, but another smell hovered just above his bunk, and Bud knew he'd never get used to that one; it was the ever present odor of despair.

The most miserable part of each day was when he woke up and thought about where he was and how long he'd have to stay here. He'd lay unmoving, while the awareness of it all came down and covered him like a sorrow-soaked shroud. So, as always, the first thought to enter Bud's head was the exact amount of time he had left to serve. On this particular morning, it amounted to eight years, two months and sixteen days. But also, on this particular morning, Bud Jones had something extra to think about and it filled him with dread. He lifted a hand and watched his fingers quiver. Today, he was scheduled for a whipping.

A small, square opening above him revealed a gray dawn sky. Bud raised up and peered through the bars. He saw a half dozen guards, carrying shotguns, exit the door of their barracks and saunter across the yard toward the cell block. Soon they would be here to line up the prisoners and march them to the dining room. Breakfast never varied: a hunk of cornbread and a cup of weak coffee. Dinnertime, they got pinto beans with the cornbread, but only water to drink. Supper was the same but every once in a while there'd be a piece of fat back in the beans. On Sundays, they'd sometimes get a worm-eaten apple to ward off the scurvy. Tucker Prison wanted them healthy enough to work. In the cot below, Zack Parker, began to cough and wheeze. Zack was dying. Bud Jones had watched him die a little bit every day. Probably, he had consumption, what with the coughing and all. Two years ago, Parker had come to Tucker a healthy, robust man. Now, although close to six feet tall, he weighed no more than a hundred and twenty pounds, with sunken eyes and protruding cheekbones. After a fit of coughing, blood would form in the corners of his mouth. Still, he worked the fields along with all the rest.

Bud swung down from his cot and quickly pulled on his prison garb: denim pants and shirt, high-top shoes, and a small-billed cotton cap. He leaned over and shook his cellmate's shoulder. "Time to get up, Zack."

Zack groaned and turned over. He lay still, for a moment, then swung his feet to the floor. He tried to rise, then sank back on the cot.

Bud took his arm and helped him to his feet. "How're you feeling?"

"Not good, Bud. If they let me, I'm goin' to see the Doc. Maybe they'll put me in the infirmary."

Bud knew they wouldn't. You had to be carried to that quack before he'd put you in the infirmary. Anyway, you weren't much better off there. Most men came out feet first.

Zack had straightened up and was staring at him. "Aw hell, Bud," he murmured. "I clean forgot."

Jones cleared his throat and said, "Don't worry about it. The bastards have whipped me before." His voice trembled in spite of the resolute words.

Zack produced a piece of leather, cut from the tongue of an old shoe, and handed it to Bud. "When the time comes, put this in your mouth. It'll keep you from bitin' your tongue." The hollow cheeks creased in a grisly grin. "I used it myself, back when I was strong and whippable."

The young man nodded and stuck it in his pocket. "Get your clothes on, they'll be after us in a minute."

The guards came and escorted all the prisoners to the dining hall. Bud sat at a long, wooden table with the bread and coffee before him. He took a bite, but couldn't manage any more. He sat with downcast gaze, contemplating his plate. Finally, Bud looked around for his brothers. Seth was seated at a corner table and James sat at a table near the door. Both were staring at their younger brother with hard, implacable eyes. Bud understood the message well enough. Be tough and enduring. There is no room for weakness in this place.

The men finished eating and filed out to the courtyard. They lined up on the hard-packed clay and were counted by the guards. The prison warden, a skinny, scarecrow of a figure, walked in front of them and regarded each man with red-rimmed, squinting eyes.

He finally sighted the boy and said, "Bud Jones. Step forward."

Bud had already placed the leather in his mouth. He took a step and was seized by two of the guards. They held him by each arm, while the warden proclaimed, "Last night, this man was talking after hours. When a guard told him to shut up, he refused to do so. He kept talking." The warden surveyed the prisoners and his lean lips parted, revealing dingy teeth. "As a reward," he said, "Mr. Jones gets to take the day off. That is, after he receives his punishment."

Bud heard a few prisoners mutter under their breath. Not many had been able to stand, let alone work, after one of these all too frequent whippings. And true, he'd spoken to the man in the adjoining cell after lights out, but the rest was a lie. When the guard told him to shut up, he'd done so. He wasn't insane. None of this mattered. It was his day for a whipping. Next week, or sooner, it would be someone else. It was done to keep them in line.

The guards hustled Bud over to a thick, upright post. They turned his back to it and bound his arms around it.

No! Wait! Something was wrong. This wasn't the way to do it. He was turned the wrong way. His back should receive the lashes, not his chest. Not his stomach. A tall, long-armed trustee emerged from the guard shack and advanced toward Bud. He held onto a wooden handle. At the end of the handle hung six rough, leather thongs, each about two inches wide and four feet long. The ends of the thongs dragged along the ground. The trustee stood in front of Bud and gave the handle a shake. The thongs twisted and separated and dark matter flew from the ends. One piece landed at Bud's feet and he saw that it was a rotten bit of skin and flesh. The trustee glanced back over his shoulder at his boss.

The warden cupped his hands around his mouth and yelled, "A hundred lashes."

Bud gaped at him in bug-eyed terror. No one had ever

taken a hundred lashes before, nor even half that many. "Noooo!" he screamed.

The trustee flipped the thongs behind him, then brought them whistling through the air. They crashed into Bud's front, leaving six bloody wounds across his chest and stomach.

Again and again the leather thongs ripped into his body, raising a bright spray of blood and eating into his flesh. He could feel his stomach wall tearing. Another lash and his stomach ripped open. H could feel his entrails give way. He looked down in horror. His guts were boiling out, a great, gray mass, streaming to the ground. He screamed again and again, "Oh, God...   Oooohhh..."

"Bud! Bud! Wake up."

Seth was holding him by the shoulder and shaking him back and forth. "It's all right. You was having a bad dream. You're all right."

The young man sat up and shook his head. He glanced about. They were all standing and looking down at him. Seth pulled him to his feet and said, "You woke us all up with your hollerin'." There was no anger in his voice.

Reese strolled passed him on his way to the horses. "It's almost daylight anyway. Let's saddle up and move out."

They headed south and watched the sun rise on their left. It glinted through the treetops, lighting up the dew-laden leaves and making them sparkle like emeralds. A dark cloud bank lay low in the west, sliced with streaks of lightning. Eventually, the men came to a dirt road, leading away to the southeast. Seth looked at Robert Reese and said, "Flat delta the rest of the way. This'll take us straight to Medford."

"Will we make it by dark?"

"If we keep goin' we'll get there by dark, or a little after."

They turned their horses eastward and started down the road. A cool breeze, bringing the smell of rain, swept up from the rear. Reese glanced over his shoulder. The clouds had drawn closer now, dark and roiling. The rumble of thunder came to his ears. He said, "We'll probably catch some rain after a while. No need to halt for that."

Seth pulled his horse alongside Bud and slapped him on the shoulder. "Better get your slicker out. It's comin' on wet."

The young man glanced at his brother. "That's all right. I like the rain."

"You doin' better now?"

No, I'm not, Bud thought. I've got a bad case of nerves, had 'em since early this morning. Probably, it was just a holdover from the nightmare, but for the first time, he felt dread at what was coming. His intuition, his perception, told him that something unforeseen was waiting in Medford, something to fear. Nonetheless, he looked at his oldest brother and gave the expected response. "Yeah Seth, the closer we get, the better I feel. And when we finish with our business, I'm gonna feel real good."

"Amen to that, little brother."

James looked over and said, "Me, too."

Snake River just nodded and stepped up the pace.

Jack Murdock entered the open doorway and said, "Well now, it would seem the entire sheriff's department is at hand."

"It is now that you're here," grumped Wilkie. "What was you waitin' for, a reveille call?"

Murdock smiled and drew up a chair. "Not my favorite bugle tune," he said.

"I bet I know which was," piped Bubba. "Charge!"

"Nor that either," replied Jack. "Truth be known, I was always partial to Taps."

Harris joined in. "Any old soldier will tell you that."

Sheriff Wilkie cracked his knuckles and said, "Okay, if we can get off the subject of bugle calls for a minute, I'd like to hear some suggestions." He was seated behind his desk. The other three men were sprawled around the table. "And just one more time, I'd like to hear a guess as to when we'll see them."

Harris tilted his hat back. "I don't think anybody's had a change of thought on that, Charlie. I say late afternoon or early tonight."

The other two nodded and Murdock said, "The latter is more likely. Even if they get here sooner, they'll halt and wait until dark."

"You think they'll try something then?" asked Bubba.

"Hard to say," answered the sheriff, "but I don't think so. They'll want to get the lay of the land first. Find out a few things."

"And where'll they go to do that?" asked Bubba.

Wilkie eyed his deputy and asked, "Where would you go if you wanted some quick information?"

"I'd come to you, Charlie."

Jack and Henry were smiling at the young deputy, while Wilkie gave him a quizzical look. "Well Bubba," he said, "Ordinarily, that'd be true, but I really think these boys will look for another source."

Black Jack stroked his drooping mustache and said. "That source would, of course, be Kate's Saloon. Information in a saloon is not always reliable, but it is plentiful. You simply have to separate the wheat from the chaff."

"All right, next question. Where are they gonna stay?"

"Kate's is generally full on a Friday night," said Harris. That leaves the two boarding houses. They could, of course, decide to sleep in the stable."

Murdock said, "Mr. Reese is a man of some refinement. I don't think he'll sleep with the horses."

Wilkie turned to his deputy. "Bubba, when we finish here, I want you to visit both boarding houses. Talk to Louella and Sadie. They know the Jones boys and they've probably heard about Reese. Tell Louella that if they try to book rooms, she's to say the house is full."

"Okay."

"Next, go to Sadie and tell her she's to hold two rooms vacant for our friends. Get the room numbers while you're there, and bring them back to me. I know Sadie limits her customers two to a room, so she's to say that these are the only rooms left. That way, Reese will have to bunk with one of his nephews. We'll know exactly where they are and how many to each room."

"Good thinking," said Murdock.

"And Bubba," continued the sheriff, "tell both those women that they are to say nothing to nobody about any of this. One loose word and they'll have me to deal with. Understood?"

"Understood."

"Tell them, also, that when they encounter these men, they're to let one of us know as soon as possible, without raising any suspicion."

"Understood," repeated the deputy.

"And one more thing. This may cause the ladies to lose a bit of income. If that happens, the county will pay for their loss."

Turning to Harris, the sheriff said, "Henry, tell Kate the same thing that Bubba's gonna tell Louella. Who knows? She may have a slow night. Now there's no need reminding Kate Mulroney to keep this confidential, but she needs to know her losses will also be covered."

"I'll tell her," said Harris.

"Dosh Colson usually reports for work in the middle of the afternoon. When he comes on, tell him to keep an eye peeled for this bunch and let us know if he spots them."

"He'd do that anyway, but I'll tell him."

"Good. Anybody feel the need to add anything? Now's the time."

Murdock fired up one of his thin cheroots and blew out smoke. "Any little morning chore for me, Charlie?"

Wilkie too a sip of coffee and smiled at his friend. "I think I'll put you to doing one of the things you're good at."

"It's a little too early for poker."

"Yes, but it's not too early to start intimidating people. I want you to circulate around. Tell folks we'd still like to have their help, but if they can't give that, they should stay away from our visitors, even if they happen to be friends. Now personally, I don't think these four have a friend in the world, but there's no accounting for taste. Inform the good citizenry that anybody seen drinking with them, or walking with them, or even talking with them, will have you to deal with. I'm sure you remember how to convey that."

Murdock blew twin streams of smoke out his nostrils. "It goes against a somewhat humble and gentle nature, but I'll do my best." Chuckles all around.

"Uh-huh," Wilkie grunted. "Anything else?"

Murdock said, "It's my opinion that Snake River Reese knows he's been acquitted. He recruited the witnesses and he would have checked with them by now. Probably, he telegraphed them in Little Rock. Therefore, for whatever it's worth, he'll come in with his nephews."

"Well, I guess that don't really matter. What does matter is how they plan to come at us."

The sheriff leaned back in his chair, withdrew a pouch

of tobacco, and filled the bowl of his pipe. He fired the tobacco, while Bubba was lighting a cigarette. The smoke from cigar, pipe, and cigarette mingled and rose to the ceiling.

"Well," said Murdock, "Robert Reese will have a plan, but that plan will go out the window when he sees there are four of us instead of two. He'll have to adapt."

"Bubba cleared his throat. "Maybe they'll just change their mind and keep on riding."

"I doubt it," answered Wilkie, "and for sure, Reese ain't gonna pass up his meeting with Harris."

"I think they will be cautions," said Murdock. "Reese has just missed going to prison. He will not want to take that chance again. And the brothers, most assuredly, will not want to risk going back to Tucker. However, each of us has given them a reason to hate us, and their caution will have its limits."

"All except me," said Bubba.

Wilkie looked at his deputy. "All except you, what?"

"They don't hate me," said Dawkins. "They don't even know me."

"That's right, they don't," said Harris. He glanced at the sheriff. "And that might be useful to us, Charlie"

"Could be," said Wilkie. "I'll consider it. Now, there's one other thing that's been on my mind and I really don't know how to get this across."

Three sets of eyes were turned toward the sheriff. He drew on his pipe and said, "There's some good people in this town, and I suppose I've come to of think of them as *my* people. When the fight starts, I'd hate for any of them to get accidentally shot, and hell, I guess I'm hoping you feel the same way."

Murdock extinguished his cigar in a tin ashtray and answered, "I think I understand, Charlie. And we'll try to watch out for them. However, I'm sure you'll agree that our self preservation comes first."

"Of course. That goes without saying."

"Because," added Black Jack, "if we go down, those same good people will be at the mercy of the Jones boys and Snake River Reese."

"Damn fine point," replied Wilkie, "and I'm through talking." He raised his eyebrows inquiringly and looked around.

"I'm off to the boarding houses," said Bubba.

"And I," said Murdock, "will speak to a few of our townsmen."

"Good," said the sheriff. "Henry, I guess you'll be seeing Katie and Dosh."

"Sure, Charlie," said Harris. "We'll see you later."

The three men rose and walked through the open doorway. Bubba went out last and closed the door behind them. Charles Wilkie sat alone at his desk, thinking and puffing on his pipe. In the dusky office, the smoke seemed to evolve into wavering images, and Charlie contemplated them through half closed eyes. There was Snake River Reese peering with undisguised malice from between the bars of a cell, and Black Jack Murdock returning his glare with a sardonic smile. Bubba Dawkins cocking a shotgun behind Donald Lacey's head, and at that particular moment, near as cold and steady as anyone could wish. And Henry Harris. Harris had helped him more than once, had even served as his deputy, bringing his gun to bear when Wilkie desperately needed that gun. He was maybe closer to Harris than he was to the others, but of the three, he understood Henry Harris least.

He knew John Murdock to be the archetypical southern aristocrat, one of the last of his kind. This was a breed who believed that, with proper provocation, you may kill a man, but you must never be rude. A product of the Old South, brought up amidst wealth and refinement, bound by its rigid code of honor. He had lost it all, lost treasure and property and a beloved wife. Now only the honor remained.

Bubba Dawkins had served as his deputy for close to a year and Wilkie had watched the young man grow and mature. What Wilkie found most appealing was Dawkin's integrity and his innate honesty. Bubba Dawkins had never learned to dissemble or deceive, and Charlie Wilkie thought this quite remarkable.

But now, he came to Henry Harris. The only insight Charlie had ever been able to achieve here was that Harris seemed to be two people enclosed in one carcass. There was the warm and friendly Henry, the kind of man people liked to stop on the street so they could tell him the latest joke. Henry would laugh and perhaps tell them a joke in return, and people would go away and say that Henry Harris was a good old boy, one of the best.

Charles Wilkie blew out smoke and nodded his head. And it would all be true, he thought, just as true as it could be. But there was another person there, and not many people had seen him. If they had, they would have quickly slipped away. Most certainly, they would not have stuck around to tell him a joke. This other person could make his appearance in a instant, and where there had been the affable Henry, there now stood Harris, the deadly gunfighter, the consummate killing machine. Charlie had seen this transformation more than once, and was shocked anew each time. Afterward, Harris would revert to his normal state and there was Henry, without any menace or the slightest sign of remorse. For a long time now, Charlie had taken the familiar Henry with a rather large measure of salt.

Wilkie tapped the ashes from his pipe, placed it on a stand, then thought, for a moment, about the Phillips County sheriff. Some doubt hovered, just at the edge of his consciousness, and maybe a little fear. He kept them at a distance, but occasionally, he heard their whispering voices. *You're getting old, Charlie. You're moving slower. Your eyesight is failing, and maybe those nerves are starting to go.*

But there was another voice which drowned out all the others, and this was the one the sheriff listened to. He was listening to it now and recognized it always as the voice of his manhood

Bullshit, the voice declared. You are Charles Harrington Wilkie, sheriff of Phillips County, and they'll have to reckon with you. Harris and Murdock are the most formidable men you've ever known, but neither they nor anybody else can do this job as well as the man sitting in this chair. The sheriff smiled a grim smile and spoke aloud, "We're all waiting for you. Come on, you bastards, and get a belly full."

If I'm the Chief Deputy, thought Bubba, why'd I get stuck with this chore? He realized why, of course. He knew these two old biddies better than anyone else, even better than the sheriff. After all, one of them was his landlady. Be that as it may, they both could make him more nervous than a couple of mean drunks on a Saturday night.

The wooden sign, stuck on a post by the street, simply read: BOARDING HOUSE. Louella Perkins had drawn a rocking chair out to the front porch, and sat watching him come up the steps.

"Mornin' Miss Perkins," said Dawkins, pausing on the top step.

"Why hello, Bubba. How's Sadie treating you?" She

never failed to ask this question, and Bubba, as always, detected a note of reproach. He figured Louella had never quite forgiven him for choosing Sadie's boarding house over her own.

"Just fine, ma'am. Caint complain."

"Well, whenever she don't, you just come on over here. I got a nice room with your name on it."

"I appreciate that," said Dawkins. He then proceeded to relay the sheriff's instructions to Louella. Surprisingly, she seemed agreeable and willing to cooperate.

"Old Charlie's got a head on his shoulders," she said. "He intends to put 'em in a small a box as possible."

"I reckon," said Bubba. "By the way, Charlie says if you get stuck with any empty rooms, the county will make it good."

Louella stopped rocking and cackled, "Tell your boss not to worry about it. I rented the last one this morning."

The deputy grinned and turned to go.

"Bubba, hold it just a minute."

Dawkins faced her and Louella leaned forward in her chair. "You just be careful out there and don't try to be no hero. You're way too young to get shot."

"Well, I sure agree with you there," said Bubba. The old lady gave a satisfied nod and resumed her rocking.

Bubba was half way up the street when it occurred to him that if Louella had rented all her rooms, then Sadie might have too. That would put a crimp in Charlie's plans. He hustled over to the other boarding house.

"No, I got three rooms left, Bubba. Why do you ask?"

Bubba couldn't resist. "Louella just told me she's full up."

Sadie, a small, trim woman with iron-gray hair, placed both hands on her hips. "Humph, if I only had six rooms, I'd be full up too. But I happen to have ten. Now, what's this all about?"

Dawkins explained and hastened to tell her about the county compensating for any loss. This, however, was not Sadie Osterman's chief concern. She wasted no time in letting her boarder know what that worry was. "So I have to let out two of my rooms to these ruffians. I hear Robert Reese is with them, so that makes three ex-cons and a killer. That's who I get to spend the night with?"

"Now Sadie, you'll be perfectly safe, and so will your other boarders. It's us they're after."

"Maybe so, but how did I deserve this honor? Why didn't Wilkie pick on Louella?"

Both Bubba and Sadie were standing in the parlor. The young man scratched his head and replied, "Well, I guess it's because I board with you. Charlie saw a chance to have one of his deputies in the same building."

Suddenly, his landlady's face softened, and she put a hand on his arm. Dawkins was surprised to see her eyes were moist. "Are you sure you know what you're getting into? Do you know what you're doing?"

"Well," he said, "as near as I can tell, I'm doing my job."

The old lady started to reply, but then her eyes filled and she turned away.

Bubba stood close, and clearing his throat said, "Sadie, when they check in, be sure and let us know. Send somebody or come yourself, but we need to know real quick."

The gray head nodded once. Bubba touched her on the shoulder, then turned and went out the door.

Black Jack Murdock passed through the saloon doors and walked over to the bar. Dosh Colson's helper, a chubby, round-faced kid, was polishing glasses, holding each one up to the light for inspection. A gangly farmer stood a few feet away. Beyond him, two townsmen shared a pitcher of beer.

"Yes sir," chirped the bartender. "What can I get for you?"

"Shot of whiskey," said Murdock

The kid poured the drink and shoved it across the bar. Jack flipped him a coin and the young man handed it back. "Dosh's orders," he said. "Your and Mr. Harris's money is no good today, or tomorrow for that matter."

"You know me then?" asked Murdock.

The bartender flashed a smile, showing perfect teeth. "I sure do, Mr. Murdock. And so does everybody else in town."

"And how did that come to pass?" asked the dark man.

"Why, because of what's about to happen," said the barkeep. "At first the whole town was asking questions back and forth. Now that they figure they know what's going on, they're just watching the players."

"Yes, I see," said Murdock. "I imagine they've come to know as much as we do. Except, like us, they don't know when the shiveree will start."

The young man nodded. He was looking at Murdock's gun.

"What's your name, son?"

"Mike, sir. Uh, Michael Mulroney."

"Mulroney. Any relation to the owner?"

"It would be distant, if at all. Mulroney's a common Irish name."

Jack nodded and lifted his glass. "Well, here's to the Irish, young Michael Mulroney. An admirable race, as evidenced by two of it's prime examples, yourself and Miss Katherine Mulroney."

Mike inclined his head and said, "Thank you, Mr. Murdock."

Lowering his voice, Jack said, "You might do me a favor in regard to the pending troubles."

An impish look, as Irish as his name, crossed the young man's face. "You mean the 'shivaree', sir?"

"Exactly."

"I'd be happy to."

"Good! If you see any unfamiliar faces, you might get word to the sheriff."

"Certainly, Mr. Murdock. The boy looked over the crowd and stated. "But unfamiliar people have been coming in all day. I reckon you know why."

"I imagine to see the showdown. Poor choice of amusement." The gaunt man shook his head.

"In your eyes, maybe, but not to them." Leaning over the bar and winking, he added, "Their usual entertainment is watching Old Bossie give birth to a calf."

Black Jack produced one of his wintry smiles and asked, "How long have you lived here?"

"All my life. My folks farm fifty acres, just west of town."

"Have you ever seen Snake River Reese?"

"Nope, heard of him, but I don't think he's ever come through Medford."

"Of course you're familiar with the Jones brothers?"

"Oh yeah. I was just a youngster when they went to prison, but I remember 'em well. Hell raisers, all of 'em. Even their daddy, old man Lucius Jones. They always ran together."

"Can you recall if anyone else ran with them, friends or other relations?"

"Not really," said the bartender, "I guess they were what you call outcasts. Didn't have any friends, didn't want any."

Murdock leaned closer. "Nobody here that would take their side in this fight?"

"I can't think of any. Of course... "

"What?"

"Well, sir, some of these people might lend the Jones boys a hand, just because they hate the sheriff, or Bubba."

"Or me and Harris," added Murdock.

"Yes, sir, that too."

"Anybody special come to mind?"

The boy shrugged. "Not anybody in particular. The sheriff has arrested a good many folks over the years, but who's to know if any of them hold a grudge."

"Still, your thought is a good one," mused Murdock. He looked about the saloon. Eight men sat at two tables in the far corner. A bottle of whiskey and glasses stood on each table. Three rough-looking field hands bellied up to the bar and Mike hurried off to serve them. As he watched, two others entered and walked to a table. Before they sat, one murmured something to the other and they both looked at Murdock. Now, the men at the other two tables were staring at him too. Jack's gaze flicked from man to man and they all looked away and resumed talking. He finished his drink and strolled out through the swinging doors. He could feel their eyes on him as he left.

Kerrie stood on a chair between the counter and rear wall, with her back toward him. She held a feather duster and was running it over a large picture frame. The picture showed a wooded range of hills, hazy with morning mist. In the foreground rose a stand of corn with green rows stretching away, and near the field, there was a house and a barn. A slim young man peered out from the house's front porch, as if watching someone approach.

Jack paused and said, "A very fine painting, Miss Kerrie. Those hills look mighty inviting."

The young woman turned and said, "Yes, they do. It's Crowley's Ridge, you know."

"You don't say. I passed through those hills on my way to Medford. Afterward, I kept looking back at them. No wonder they look familiar."

"Did you pass that farm?" she asked.

"No, ma'am, but I imagine it belongs to one Henry Harris."

"How did you know?"

"Well, the man on the porch has a familiar look."

"Miss Katie painted this."

"I assumed as much," replied Jack. He kept watching more men, and an occasional woman, walk into the saloon. The anthracite eyes followed them through the doors.

"Sometimes Miss Katie goes out there to check on Henry." She glanced at Murdock. "I hope I'm not speaking out of school."

It took a moment for him to focus again "Certainly not," he replied. "I believe that relationship is known to us all." Jack eyed Kate's assistant and added, "Speaking of relationships, I was wondering...

"Kerrie looked at him and smiled. "He walked me home last night."

"Well, good for Bubba. I figured he'd finally take action."

Kerrie blushed and said, "Well, I'm afraid I had to do a little pushing. He certainly is shy."

Two more men strode past Murdock and both gave him a hard look. He watched them walk through the swinging doors. "Do you know those last two men, Miss Kerrie?"

"Not personally. Once, they got rowdy in the saloon. Charlie and Bubba came in and escorted them out."

"Did they arrest them."

"I don't think so. I believe Charlie kicked them out of town. Come to think of it, this is the first time I've seen them back."

Suddenly, Murdock realized what he needed to do. He tipped his hat to Kerrie and said, "I believe I'll return to the saloon for a moment. By the way," he said over his shoulder, "I consider Bubba Dawkins a very lucky man."

"Thank you," she called. The gaunt figure lifted a hand in acknowledgment as he passed back through the doors.

Murdock walked over to the piano player, who was making a feeble attempt at "Sweet Betsy From Pike." He tapped the musician on the shoulder. The man looked up and Jack made a cutting motion with his hand. The man stopped playing. A few people looked over at Jack. He placed two fingers between his lips and gave out a shrill whistle. All conversation ceased instantly and everyone turned to stare at the dark stranger.

Jack cupped a thumb in his belt, and in a deep, clear voice said, "I am John Murdock, Black Jack Murdock, and I wish to make an announcement." His dark eyes swept the crowd, lingering now and then on an individual face. "Some of you may know me, and most will know why I'm here. The reason for my presence is to help a few friends with some trouble they're having. That trouble takes the form of three felons named Jones, and a gunslinger who goes by the handle of Snake River Reese." Again the sweeping gaze, and now the black look of John Murdock was there for all to see. He raised his voice a notch.

"Do these buzzards have friends here? If so, let those friends step forward." No one moved, and Murdock repeated, "If you feel you owe allegiance to these men, step forward." A slight pause. "But before you take that first step, make sure you have a weapon in your hand."

He met the gaze of several men and each one looked away. "Your sheriff believes that this Jones bunch and their uncle, Robert Reese, haven't a friend in the world. I tend to agree since I know them to be varlets and skunks of the first water, four pieces of trash, which my companions and I intend to sweep away." Another pause. Every eye in the place was on him. "Does anyone disagree with me? If so, now is the time to speak up."

Black Jack finally nodded and said, "Sheriff Wilkie is evidently correct. These misfits have no friends."

He walked among them, addressing an individual here and there, the ebony eyes boring in. "Greet them with silence," he demanded. "Show your backs to them. Shun them."

Mike, the bartender, watched Murdock like a mesmerized mouse, staring at a cobra. He tore his eyes away, glanced at the wall clock, and saw that it was almost two o'clock. He sure had a story for Dosh Colson.

Murdock reached the exit, turned back to the crowd, and said, "A very pleasant day to you all."

The crowd started to move again and a loud murmur arose. The piano player placed two trembling hands on the keys and resumed his homage to "Sweet Betsy." He sounded worse than ever.

Kate and Harris moved back from the swinging doors, just before Murdock emerged. They'd seen the whole thing and heard every word. Harris greeted his fellow deputy with a smile. Kate seemed to have been struck dumb. She stared at Jack with slightly parted lips.

Murdock stopped before them and Harris said, "Well Jack, I suppose you got Charlie's message across, but I was hoping you'd be more direct."

Jack gave a soft chuckle and replied, "You are undoubtedly correct, Henry. Evasiveness. Forbearance. They have always been my weakness."

Kate's gaze still rested on Murdock. She said, "The only way that message could be more direct would be if you wrote it on a scrap of paper and nailed it to their foreheads. I've never seen anything like it."

"Well," said Murdock, "doing it this way saved a lot of time."

"Sort of a public address," said Henry.

"Precisely. Now, if you two will excuse me, I think I'll take a nap." Jack was halfway up the stairs, when he turned and said, "Perhaps later, you two will join me for a drink." Kate and Henry nodded their heads. At this particular moment, it seemed wise to humor Black Jack.

They walked into the restaurant and Henry paused by a table. "It's past noon," he said, "you ready to eat something?"

"Maybe I'll have a sandwich, but not here. Come on back to the kitchen." She led him through a passage at the rear and Henry found himself surrounded by stoves and counters. A small table covered in a red-checked cloth, sat in a corner. They walked over and sat down.

Pete Morales, the cook, and Marge Blackwell were huddled at a counter, going over menus. Henry waved to them both and reflected that Morales, Katie's cook from day one, never seemed to age. The slim, little Mexican retained the same unlined face and sparkling eye. His movements were swift and sure and his aspect always friendly. In one way only had he changed. Pete had started off as a very good cook. Now he was a superb one. Other restaurant owners and boarding house proprietors constantly tried to woo him away from Katie.

"*Buenas tardes, Señor* Harris," he called from across the room. "*Que paso?*" Marge looked up and smiled.

"Doing all right, Pedro," he replied. "*Como esta¿*"

The small cook gave a dismissive shaking of his fingers and returned to studying the menu. Marge came over to take their order.

"Any of the meat loaf left?" asked Katie.

"Sure thing, Miss Kate."

"How about a meat loaf sandwich." She looked at Henry. "You should try it. It's pretty good."

"You talked me into it," said Henry.

Marge went away and quickly returned with two thick sandwiches.

Between bites, Harris mumbled, "This should hold us until we meet Black Jack for dinner."

Kate looked up from her sandwich and asked, "How'd he do that? I mean some of those fellows were pretty tough customers. How'd he control them that way?"

"I don't know. Charlie has told me some stories about him. You know, they were once deputies together. Anyway, some of Charlie's tales make this seem kinda tame."

"Tame? My God, Henry, he taunted them, he challenged them all, and not one so much as raised his voice."

"Yeah, I know."

"So how did they come to fear him? What did they see? I'd really like to know."

"Well Katie, I reckon they saw Black Jack Murdock with the bark on."

"And what is that, exactly?"

Harris shook his head and murmured, "One of kind, Katie. One of a kind."

Chapter Seven

Charles Wilkie looked up to see Harris coming through the door. "Where you been?" he growled.

"Well, after eating with Katie, I decided Jack had a real good idea, so I did the same thing."

"What was that?" asked Wilkie

"I went and took a nap."

"Well," said Charlie, "I hate to see you two so tensed up. Why don't you try and relax."

Henry grinned and asked, "You heard anything?"

"Nah, I think what it boils down to is, we can expect them when we see them. Did you tell Katie about the rooms?"

"No need to. She was full up by noon. She'll let us know if she sees them."

Wilkie pulled out his pocket watch. "It's near three o'clock. I imagine Dosh will be coming on duty."

"Yeah," said Harris, "I'll drop by and give him the word."

"If he sees any of 'em, he can send a message by one of Kate's workers."

"Right," said Henry. "By the way, Murdock was in the saloon earlier. Did you hear about his announcement?"

"Announcement? What the hell are you talkin' about, Harris?"

"Well, he was just following your orders, I guess." Harris proceeded to tell Wilkie about the scene in Kate's saloon."

"Wilkie grinned and said, "The one and only Murdock."

"Yeah."

"Well, I guess he was trying to save some time."

"That's what he said," replied Henry. Charlie's soft laughter followed him out the door.

Halfway to the saloon, he met Bubba Dawkins. The deputy approached at a stiff walk, as if his joints were locking up. He drew out a handkerchief and wiped the sweat from his face, a face, Henry noted, that had lost some of its color. Dawkins greeted Harris and hitched at his gun belt.

Harris gently asked, "How are you feeling, Bubba?"

Being Bubba, he replied, "My nerves are acting up, Henry. Y'all better keep an eye on me."

"No need for that. You'll do all right. Just remember, you've got some good help."

"I know it, but I keep wondering what they're gonna do after we face up to them."

"Ah, that's the secret, deputy," came a voice from the sidewalk. John Murdock was leaning against a wooden building, one thin leg crossed over the other. He straightened and walked over to the two men. "Never concern yourself with the outcome of your deeds," he said. "What you perceive as bravery in most men is simply their knack of ignoring the consequences."

"Easier said than done," said Dawkins.

"Quite so," replied Murdock. He slapped Bubba on the shoulder and added, "but you keep working on it."

"Where you headed?" asked Harris.

"I'm on my way to see the High Sheriff." Glancing at Dawkins, he said, "I will suggest to him that we have one last get together, say about five o'clock."

Henry looked at Murdock with new appreciation. Jack realized that only Bubba needed this meeting. He would draw essential strength from the others. "Sounds good to me," he said.

Murdock nodded and headed down the street. Bubba watched the raw-boned figure with the jack-knifing legs and said, "I'll bet Jack don't go over a hundred and thirty pounds."

"Yeah," said Henry. "Same weight as a cougar."

Dawkins continued his rounds and Henry walked to Kate's Place. He entered the saloon and caught Dosh Colson's eye. The bartender came over and Harris said, "You might be the first to see our visitors. Get word to us as soon as you can."

"I will," said Dosh. "Hey, did you hear what Murdock done?"

"Sure did."

The bartender gave him a measured look. "With you two around, it won't take long for things to heat up." Harris nodded and headed toward the door.

Young Mike Mulroney came out the storeroom and stood beside his boss. They both watched Harris walk away. He was still within ear shot when Dosh turned to the boy and said, "You know, everybody's talking about Black Jack Murdock, but there goes the Jones's worst nightmare. And probably Reese's, too. I wonder if any of 'em know it."

* * *

Sometime after five o'clock, Wilkie and his fellow lawmen watched a west wind sweep across Medford. Behind it, dark rain clouds gathered and billowed. The wind blew up Main Street and swirled dust around the four men. They were gathered in front of the sheriff's office, and as they stood there, the cloud bank swallowed up the sun and an instant gloom descended. Medford's citizens began to leave the sidewalks, heading for their homes to avoid the coming storm. A lone horseman trotted up the street and four sets of eyes watched him approach.

"It's Lonnie Sims," said Wilkie. "He farms some land just west of here."

Sims reined up and patted the sweating animal, a large dray horse, unsuited for any gait other than a walk. The rider, a thin-faced man, worn by hard labor, got right to the point. "Charlie, there's four men holed up not far from here. I seen 'em on the way in. Could be the ones you're expectin'."

"What did they look like?"

"I passed some distance from 'em, but three of 'em looked kinda like the Jones boys. 'Course, it's been awhile. I caint be sure."

"What about the other one?"

"Trim sort of a fellow, if you know what I mean. Kinda duded up. He wore a gun. They all did, but his was slung low and tied down.

"Do you think they saw you?" asked Harris.

"If I saw them, I reckon they saw me, too."

The farmer rode on and Murdock said, "Well Henry, perhaps we should postpone that drink with Miss Kate."

"I'll tell her," said Harris.

Wilkie gazed down the street and murmured, "Looks like the talking is over."

"Good," replied Murdock. "Charlie, I don't wish to offend, but your meetings were growing a bit tiresome."

Wilkie didn't mention that Jack had suggested the last one. He glanced to the west and said, "Okay, this weather has answered one question. They ain't gonna spend the night getting wet. We'll go as planned. John, you and me will start our rounds at the north end of town. Henry and Bubba will begin at the other end, and we'll cross at the middle. Everybody keeps patrolling until our visitors show up."

The sheriff watched Bubba and Henry walk away, one on each side of the street. He and Murdock started in the other direction. Before crossing the street, Murdock turned to him and said: "Just like old times, eh, Charlie?"

Wilkie responded with a wry grin. "Yeah, old times and younger men."

"Speak for yourself, sheriff. I'm still in my prime."

Charlie watched the lean figure stalk away, before continuing up his side of the street. The four came together twice, while making their rounds. Before the third encounter, darkness had come down, and lanterns and lamps were glowing all over Medford. Wilkie stood with his friends under an unlit porch canopy and they watched the storm clouds roll in. Lightning forked out beneath them, followed by instant claps of thunder. Then the clouds swept over the town and released their burden of rain. The water came down in torrents, hammering on the tin roofs and swaying in solemn sheets across Main Street. The street intersected another avenue at this point and the sheriff saw Harris turn and peer down its westward length. Darkness and the heavy rain made seeing difficult, but he figured those sharp eyes had detected movement. Wilkie signaled the other two and they all stood watching. Suddenly, four riders appeared through the downpour and came on at a walk. Their clothing was drenched and their wide-brimmed hats drooped down over their faces. Still, there was no doubt in anybody's mind who they were. The Jones brothers, along with their Uncle Robert, had at last arrived in Medford.

The horsemen came to the intersection, wheeled to the right, and headed south on Main Street. They stopped in front of Kate's Place, dismounted, and stood for a moment in the entrance lamp's glow. Before going inside, one of them removed his hat and brushed away the moisture.

"Snake River Reese," said Charlie.

Bubba exhaled loudly and said, "They never saw us."

"Yeah," said Charlie. "Too dark in here. Let's wait a minute."

The men stepped back into deeper darkness and Bubba fumbled with his tobacco pouch. Henry touched him on the arm and said, "Don't strike a match." Bubba nodded and returned the pouch to his pocket. Their gaze remained fixed on the hotel door.

Kate was standing behind the check-in counter when the four men came in, dripping water on her hardwood floor. One had removed his hat, and as they approached, he gave her a thin-lipped smile. It did not touch his pale, expressionless eyes.

"Good evening," he said. "We're in need of a couple of rooms."

Kate looked at each one in turn, then said, "I'm afraid we're full up. Usually happens on a Friday night."

"I see. Are there rooms available elsewhere?"

"Well, you might try one of the boarding houses. We have two here."

"Which one offers the most rooms?" asked Reese.

"That would be Sadie's place." She glanced at the three men standing behind him. "Of course, you Jones boys already know that."

"So I see your remember us," said Seth.

"You're not the kind we forget."

James edged around his uncle and said, "What's that supposed to mean?"

Reese fixed his nephew with a stare, then returned his attention to Kate. "Pay no mind to James. We're all a mite tired and more than a little wet."

Kate was not to be deterred. She glanced at James and said, "It means you Joneses are trouble. Always have been and always will be."

"Is that why you're refusing us the rooms?" asked Reese.

"No, I was telling you the truth about being full. By the way, who might you be?"

Katie knew, of course, but she wanted to see if Reese would identify himself. Snake River promptly did just that.

"My name is Robert Reese, and I'm uncle to these boys. You, of course, are Miss Katherine Mulroney."

Kate was momentarily flustered by the man's mild speech and good manners. Here was one to be reckoned with, she thought. "Yes, I'm Kate Mulroney. Sorry we can't accommodate you."

"Quite all right, Miss Mulroney." Reese replaced his hat and headed for the entrance. The three nephews followed him, and from their spot at the door, James Jones turned and gave her a venomous stare.

Charlie and his deputies watched the men mount up and ride over to Sadie's. They remained inside, for a bit, then emerged and led their horses across the street to the livery stable. Then all four walked back and reentered the boarding house.

"Looks like they got the two rooms," said Bubba.

"Yeah," said Wilkie. "I saw Sadie a little while ago. Their rooms are on either side of yours."

"Now that's real comforting, Charlie. Thanks for telling me."

The men smiled and Jack said, "Well, Bubba, perhaps you'll hear something through the walls."

Henry laid a hand on Dawkins' shoulder. "Maybe he won't have to listen through a wall," he said. He looked at the sheriff. "Remember Charlie, as far as we know, they still think Dick's your deputy. None of them have laid eyes on Bubba."

Wilkie eyed his deputy and said, "What time does Sadie put out the supper?"

"Seven o'clock, right on the dot." Bubba stepped out of the shadows and pulled out his pocket watch. "That'll be about thirty minutes from now."

"How many of her other boarders know you're a deputy?"

"Well, I don't know. Depends on who's checked out and who's checked in today. There's two, been there all week. They know, but they may have left. I'd have to talk to Sadie."

"Okay," said Charlie, "go on over see her. Find out how the land lays and make sure she don't give you away. Also make perfectly sure nobody at that table is gonna recognize you." He glanced once more at the boarding house and added, "It's breaking one of our rules 'cause you'll be alone with them. What do you think?"

Bubba forced a smile and said, "It's okay. Hell, it's better than just standing here waiting."

"In that case," said Wilkie, "I guess you're having supper with our friends."

Murdock said, "If you get to talking to them, you might, in a subtle way of course, say a few words about the sheriff. That ought to open them up."

Dawkins peered at Murdock and asked, "What does *subtle* mean?"

Murdock stroked his chin and answered, "It means in a perspicacious manner, my boy. Er, that is to say . . ."

"He means go at it round about," explained Henry.

"Oh," responded Bubba.

Wilkie gave his deputy a long stare and Bubba said, "Don't worry Charlie. I can handle it."

The sheriff cleared his throat and said, "Okay, be on your way then."

Charlie, Henry, and Jack watched their companion walk away to Sadie's. Bubba paused in front of the entrance, pulled out a red bandanna, and wiped the moisture from his face. He opened the front door, glanced back down the street, and disappeared inside.

Harris turned to Wilkie. "Feeling better about your deputy?"

"He's coming along," grunted Wilkie.

In a soft voice, Henry murmured, "Yep, coming along just fine."

"I don't think we have to be overly worried about him," said the sheriff. "Even if that bunch discovers who he is, they won't dare gun him in front of all those upstanding boarders, not to mention Miss Sadie."

"You're probably right," said Murdock, "but we ought to be wary of assigning practical, or even sensible behavior, to these low lifes."

"Good point," answered Wilkie. "Let's get a little closer, case he needs us in a hurry."

The three men walked toward the boarding house. Wilkie strolled past and paused beside a dogwood tree. Jack had already stopped at the north corner of the building and was standing to the side of a lamp-lit window. He looked at Wilkie and both men nodded. Harris crossed the street, halted abreast of the boarding house entrance, and backed into the shadows of an empty shed. At the moment, they were the only humans in sight. They waited.

Bubba closed the front door behind him and quickly glanced around.

The parlor was unoccupied, nobody on the stairway. The doors to the four rooms on the bottom floor were shut tight. Bubba approached the nearest door and tapped softly.

"Who is it?" came a voice from within.

"It's me, Sadie. Bubba. Open the door."

The door swung back immediately and his landlady stood before him in a full length dress and floral hat. She grabbed Bubba by the arm and pulled him into the room. "Oh Bubba," she gasped. "I was just leaving to tell the sheriff." She took a deep breath, blew it out, and exclaimed, "There're here. I just now checked them in."

Dawkins put a finger to his lips and said, "Shh! I know they're here. We've been watching them."

"Oh, good," she said. "I need to get supper on the table. My cook left early and I've got to do it myself." She removed her hat, laid it on a table, and started for the door. Bubba caught her by the elbow and Sadie swung around to face him. Her face was flushed and her lower lip was trembling.

Bubba said, "Wait a minute. We need to talk about something. Now try to calm down."

"Calm down," she exclaimed. "How can I calm down when—"

"Sadie, lower your voice." This time his tone was firmer.

"When my house is filled with cutthroats," she finished in a whisper.

"How many boarders do you have besides Reese and the Jones boys?"

"Three," she answered.

"How many will be here for supper?"

"Just two, besides the outlaws. Jimmy Smythe is over at Kate's. He eats there every Friday night, then stays to play poker."

"Good," said Bubba. "Jimmy knows me."

Sadie gave him a quizzical look. "What difference does that make?"

Ignoring the question, Bubba asked, "Do the other two know me?"

"I don't think so. Just two drummers from out of town. They both checked in today." Cocking her head sideways and eyeing Dawkins, Sadie said, "Bubba, what's going on?"

Bubba led her to the sofa, sat her down, and told her of his assignment. Sadie swallowed and said, "Don't do it, Bubba. It's too dangerous."

"Don't worry about me. I'll be okay."

"Then think about me," she said. "I don't think my heart can take it."

Bubba placed a hand on her shoulder. "You'll be okay, too."

"Well, I know one thing. After I lay out the food, I'm going to eat in the kitchen."

Dawkins was first into the dining room. He took one of the wooden chairs, and had barely settled into it when he heard men's voices coming down the hallway. He hitched his chair closer to the table, looked down, and to his horror, discovered he was still wearing his badge. He ripped it off and was stuffing it into his shirt pocket when the first diner entered.

"How do," said the plump salesman. He was dressed in a brown, plaid suit and wore an outsized ring on his left pinkie. "About time for supper, ain't it?"

"Pretty near," answered Dawkins.

The drummer held out a soft, smooth hand and Bubba shook it. "Frank Lovett," he said, giving the deputy a gold-toothed smile. "Salesman by trade. Liquor's my line, everything from premium whiskey to French champagne."

"Name's Bud Hawkins," said Bubba. "Just a farmer, in town to do a little trading."

"Not *just,* my lad," exclaimed Lovett. "Not by a damn sight. Salt of the earth, farmers. Why, where would we be without them?"

"Without food or clothing, for one thing," came a voice from the doorway. The second salesman walked in and took a seat. He, too, wore a suit and tie, but the tie looked frayed, and his coat was shiny at the elbows. Nodding to Dawkins, he said, "Name's Frazier, purveyor of kitchen condiments."

Bubba surmised from his appearance that pepper, salt, and cinnamon powder didn't move as well as liquor. "Bud Hawkins," he murmured. Sadie followed Frazier into the room, bearing a tray of biscuits. She moved in and out quickly, bringing fried chicken, creamed potatoes, and a steaming pot of coffee. All the time, she kept glancing out the door or looking over her shoulder. She darted out again and they could hear her calling, "Gentlemen, supper's on the table."

Two upstairs doors opened and closed and Bubba heard heavy boots descending the stairway. The Jones brothers entered first, peering around the room. Bubba, going by age, identified each one immediately. Seth, obviously the oldest, stared at Dawkins, then glanced at the two drummers. He sported a full-length beard like his brothers, and like theirs, his hair hung to his shoulders. All were lanky and tall and bore signs of hard travel, their clothing grimy and wrinkled. As they took a seat, Bubba's nose caught the familiar scent of horse and human sweat. Without a word to anyone, they reached for the victuals and began eating. Both salesman ducked their heads, then glanced at each other. Bubba kept a stealthy lookout for Snake River Reese, and suddenly, there he stood in the open doorway.

"Good evening, gentleman." Giving his nephews a rueful glance, he added, "I hope we haven't delayed your supper."

The first salesman said, "Not at all, sir. Please join us."

Bubba watched the gunfighter advance toward the table and take a seat. He'd never seen a man move so gracefully, like a big prowling at. He noticed, also, that Reese, unlike the Jones boys, still wore his gun.

The salesmen, Bubba, and Reese all introduced themselves, and Reese said, "These are my nephews." The brothers, constantly reaching and chewing, said nothing. Seth occasionally glanced at Bubba.

The liquor salesman said, "I'd have gladly contributed a bottle of my stock to this occasion, but Miss Sadie has forbidden it. Pity, too. I was looking forward to a glass of wine with my supper." The brothers stopped gobbling and looked at Lovett with a newly awakened interest.

"We don't drink," said Reese, and his nephews dropped their heads and started eating again.

Lovett looked up in surprise. "Not any of you?" he asked.

"No."

"Not ever?"

"I'm afraid not," said Reese.

The salesman shook his head in bewilderment and gnawed on a drumstick. Through a mouthful of chicken, he asked, "Are you gentlemen citizens of Medford?"

"No. The boys, here, once owned some land out on Crowley's Ridge, but they lost it."

"Sorry to hear it," said Lovett.

Seth peered, once more, at Bubba Dawkins and said, "Don't I know you?"

Bubba waited a moment, pretending to swallow some food. When he felt his voice was under control, he responded, "Could be. My daddy and me has got a farm, down the road a ways."

Seth shook his hair back and resumed eating.

Bubba glanced around and saw Reese staring at him. The gunfighter took a sip of coffee and said, "Mr. Hawkins, I imagine you know most of the townspeople."

"I reckon," said Bubba.

"My nephews were wondering if Medford employs the same officials. For instance, does Mayor Matthew Harper still hold that office?" The two drummers gave each other a puzzled look, probably wondering why the brothers didn't speak for themselves.

"Sure does," said Bubba. "I guess nobody else wants it."

"And the sheriff. I believe his name was Wilkie?"

"Still here."

"I suppose nobody wants that job either."

Bubba felt his throat tighten. "No, someone runs against him every two years, but he always wins. I guess the town knows when they've got a good one."

"What's good about him?" growled James.

Bubba's eyes darted to the speaker. "Well, he's about as brave as they come, and he knows how to keep order."

"He's also a low-down sneak," said the brother.

"I wonder," said Bubba, "why you'd say such a thing."

James's chair scraped back and he began to rise. Robert Reese shook his head and the nephew sank back down. All three brothers were now glaring at Bubba. He felt the force of their hatred, and with it came an understanding of their terrible resolve. They were here to kill and there would be no faltering or turning away. Neither, of course, would Bubba's comrades, the most implacable men he had ever known. The men were fated to meet and Bubba's mind recoiled from the finality of it all. His pulse pounded in his ears and his vision blurred, and through it all, he could hear the soft voice of Snake River Reese.

"And Wilkie's deputy. I'm told his name is Dick Wessell. How does he fare?"

Something's wrong here, thought Bubba. I'm the one supposed to be getting information. Instead, I'm the one giving it. Reese held him in his gaze, and Dawkins, for the first time, noticed the blanched, almost colorless eyes, a viper's eyes. Bubba stared into them like a captivated frog. He gave a quick shake of his head and replied, "Dick's doing okay. They make a good team."

The ashen eyes widened slightly and Bubba was captured once more.

Leave me alone, he thought. Just leave me alone.

"And Henry Harris," came the silky voice. "Is Henry Harris nearby?"

The deputy heard the name and a familiar figure rose up in his mind. And with that image came a flooding recollection of the deadly skill and utter competence of Henry Harris. Bubba's dread, along with Reese's spell, began to float away like strands of gossamer. He lifted his head. The Jones brothers continued to eye him like savage wolves and Reese's gaze remained fixed, but Bubba Dawkins felt fresh courage rise and surge within him. He looked upon the Denver Gunfighter and thought, Oh, don't worry about Harris. He's nearby, and he's not likely to leave. He'll be waiting for you like everyman's Death.

Bubba faced toward the Jones boys and returned their feral stare. And for you, there'll be a sheriff named Charles Wilkie. He's maybe a little old and he's had to let his belt out a few notches, but he's still solid grit and all nerve. Try him.

Try him like Donald Lacey did, and watch him grind you up, watch him diminish you.

Oh, and by the way, there's someone else you'll get to meet. I don't think you've met him before, although your uncle has. Ask him about John Murdock, but don't expect Reese to describe or explain him, because nobody can. Black, Black Jack Murdock, the dark and fatal enemy you sometimes see in nightmares.

And yet, he's my friend, thought Bubba Dawkins, as they all are, and I swear to God I will not let them down. He leveled his gaze at Reese and said, "Why do you ask about Harris's whereabouts?"

"He's askin' because he wants to know," said the youngest Jones.

Reese looked at Bud and held up a placating hand. "My nephews are worn down from the trail," he said. "A good night's sleep in a real bed will fix them up."

Dawkins shrugged and Reese said, "To answer your question, I'm merely curious about the man. They say he's good with a gun, one of the best."

"I understand he's retired," said Bubba.

"Word is, he's simply changed occupations. I hear he's a farmer now."

"Why, that's what this fellow is," exclaimed Lovett.

"Is that so?" said Reese. "Is your farm close to his?"

Bubba decided to turn this around. "No offense, Mr. Reese, but you seem uncommonly interested in Harris."

"Oh, simply curiosity, as I said."

"And what is it you do for a living?"

Reese smiled and said, "For a living? Well, I suppose I do things that insure I go on living."

James snickered and reached for the biscuits. He and his brothers settled back and resumed eating. Watching them, Bubba asked, "Are you gentlemen just passing through?"

All three continued to munch and Bubba began to think they would ignore him. Finally, Seth lifted his head and said, "Nope, this is our home, or at least it used to be."

"It seems my nephew—" Reese began, but this time it was Seth who held up the restraining hand.

"We were arrested by that sheriff you think so highly of, snatched from our father's freshly dug grave, and rail-roaded by him and a jury to ten years in Tucker Prison." Seth stared at Bubba and said, "Maybe you remember the trial."

"No," said Bubba. "I couldn't have been more than ten or eleven at the time, and daddy didn't bring me to town much."

"Bud here was sixteen," said Seth, but he got the same ten years.

Bubba tried to sound sympathetic. "That's a shame," he said. "But I hope you boys ain't holding a grudge."

"What's that to you?" asked Bud.

The first salesman cleared his throat and rose from the table. "Excuse me, gentlemen. I'll believe I'll retire." The second salesman also rose and quickly followed him out the door.

"Oh, it's nothing to me," answered Bubba.

"Maybe you figure on running to Wilkie?"

"Not me. I'm heading back to my farm." With this, Bubba wiped his mouth with a napkin and stood up from the chair.

"It took three of them, you know." Seth was speaking again. "Wilkie and Wessell and that gunslinger, Henry Harris."

Bubba nodded and stepped away from the table, figuring anything else he said would only antagonize them. He was almost to the door, when it swung open and Jimmy Smythe, Sadie's absent border, strode into the room. "Damn, Bubba," he exclaimed. "You and Wilkie need to check out that poker game. I played for an hour and never won a pot."

Chapter Eight

Everything slowed down for Bubba Dawkins. Jimmy seemed to move toward him like a man wading through waist high water. He turned back toward the table and saw the four men look at each other. They spoke, but the words sounded muffled and hollow, like echoes in a cave.

Smythe noticed the other diners. He started to say something else to Bubba, then stopped and stood there with an awful recognition dawning on his face. Snake River Reese spoke and everything came back into focus.

"Do you know us?" Reese asked the boarder.

Smythe's gazed into the eyes of the gunfighter. His mouth remained open but nothing came out. He seemed entranced, and Bubba imagined that he himself had borne that same look a few minutes ago. Reese shifted in his chair and the gun became visible. "I asked you if you knew us."

"I think so," muttered Smythe.

"Who are we?"

"Well sir, I believe you're Mr. Robert Reese, and these are the, uh, the Jones brothers."

"And who is this man?" asked Reese.

"Why he's...he's..." Jimmy turned an agonized gaze toward Bubba.

"Go ahead, Jimmy," said Dawkins.

"He's Bubba Dawkins."

"Bud Hawkins, hell," shouted Seth, rising from his seat. "I knew I'd seen him before. Little Bubba Dawkins, old man Jacob Dawkins' son."

Sadie Osterman, appeared in the doorway, and in a quavering voice, asked, "Is something the matter, gentlemen? I heard loud voices."

"It's all right, Sadie," said Dawkins. "Go back to the kitchen."

"Go back to— *Oh*. Oh, yes," said Sadie. "I clean forgot. I'm fixing cobbler for dessert." The old lady turned and hurried from the room, but cobbler was the last thing on her mind. Once out of sight, she quickly slipped out the front door.

Seth Jones remained standing. Then Robert Reese rose from his chair, along with James and Bud. All four of them stood and stared at Bubba and Jimmy.

Again, Reese addressed Smythe in that relentless voice. "And would Mr. Dawkins be a lawman? Would he happen to be the sheriff's deputy?"

The boarder's stricken face turned once more to Bubba. The deputy saw the terror written there, and felt a rush of anger toward the ones who'd caused it. "Jimmy," he said, "go on up to your room. This don't concern you."

No one objected as Smythe bolted from the dining room. Bubba turned to the men and felt fear and weakness returning. Nevertheless, he managed to look Reese in the eye. "Why don't you ask me?"

"Very well," said the gunfighter. "Did you lie to us? Are you here to spy on us? Are you Wilkie's deputy?"

"Hell, them are easy ones," came a new voice from the hallway.

Reese's head snapped around as Charles Wilkie walked into the room. "Well, go ahead, Bubba. Answer Mr. Reese's questions."

The young deputy's nerve returned anew, and for a brief moment, Bubba Dawkins loved Charlie as much as he'd ever loved his own father.

Instead of making a reply, he slowly, and with steady fingers, pulled the badge from his pocket and pinned it to his shirt. A low growl came from one of the Jones boys, and Bubba gave them all a grim smile.

"Just wait," said Bud in a choked voice. "Just wait."

"Robert," intoned Wilkie, "is that young man threatening us? Because, if he's threatening us, that would put him in violation of the law."

"Shut up, Bud," snapped Reese. Then to Wilkie, "As you can see, Sheriff, these boys are unarmed and in no position to threaten anybody."

"So is my deputy," said Charlie.

"Why that's right, Wilkie," came the purring voice. "Looks like you and I are the only one's heeled. I wonder if you'd like to..."

Suddenly, Reese's pallid eyes flitted back to the doorway. Just outside stood Henry Harris. Behind him, Reese could make out another figure, half hidden in the shadows.

"It's Harris," exclaimed Seth Jones, as Henry walked in and stood beside the sheriff.

Bubba felt his courage mount another notch. He'd been alone and in peril. Now the cavalry was here. He looked at Reese, but the gunfighter had eyes only for Henry Harris. The two men stared at each other and finally Reese said, "I've looked forward to meeting you, Mr. Harris. As a matter of fact, I've come all this way to see you."

Harris might as well have been observing a quilting bee. His face revealed nothing. Without speaking, he stepped away from Wilkie and stood with feet slightly spread, his gun hand loosely hanging. Bubba looked at him and his mouth dropped open. The friendly companion he'd known was no longer there. In the blink of an eye, he had become something else, something fearful and fatal.

Reese regarded Harris and smiled. "Not tonight, I'm afraid, especially with you wearing that badge. Perhaps we could have our interview tomorrow morning."

Henry spoke for the first time. "That's up to you, but I'll still be wearing this badge."

"Yes, well it doesn't really matter. So will the sheriff and Mr. Dawkins, and they have an interview also, uh, with my nephews." He glanced back at the doorway, but the shadowy figure was gone. "Now, I think we'll finish our supper."

Reese sat back down and his nephews slowly followed his example.

Henry walked over and stood with his back to the sheriff. Bubba and Charlie headed through the door and Henry backed out behind them. All the time, he was looking at Reese.

They found Murdock on the front porch, leaning against a railing. Sadie Osterman stood beside him. Charlie said, "Thanks, Sadie. You did the right thing."

"When the shouting started, I figured Bubba needed help." She put a hand on Wilkie's arm. "What happened in there, Charlie?"

"Not much. Just a little talk. There shouldn't be any more trouble tonight."

"Well, I don't care what you say, Charles Wilkie. This is their last night in my place, and that's final."

The sheriff patted her on the shoulder and said, "All right. Now you better get back inside."

"I'm going, but I'll wait in the kitchen. I'll clean the table after they're back in their rooms." The old lady hitched up her skirts and went inside.

The sheriff and his deputies walked back toward the jail. The rain had stopped and a few stars glimmered between the clouds. A warm wind blew at their backs and set a street lantern swinging. They entered the office and Bubba put on a pot of coffee. Everyone took a seat at the table.

"Well, what do you think?" said the sheriff, to no one in particular.

"I think," said Harris, "that the next time we see them, they'll all have their guns on."

Wilkie nodded. "And according to Mr. Reese, that'll be tomorrow morning."

"No chance of them coming out tonight?" asked Bubba.

"I don't think so." the sheriff said. "I considered posting guards on the boarding house, but my gut feeling is they'll stay where they are. He got up and returned with cups and a coffee pot. "They thought there were two. Now they see that we're probably four. The odds have evened out. They'll need to talk about that. Besides, we're patrolling till twelve, and after that, we're the ones who'd have to do the guarding. I think it's more important to rest and be fresh for what's sure to come tomorrow. He turned to Murdock and asked, "Did they see you, Jack?"

"Snake River saw someone standing behind Henry, but I don't think he recognized me. He probably assumed it was Dick Wessell."

"Yeah, well you did right in staying where you were. That's one little surprise they've still got coming."

"So what do we do now?" asked Bubba.

Charlie sipped his coffee and thought a moment. Finally, he looked up and said, "We only got two prisoners, so there's four extra cots. We can drag 'em out of the cells and sleep here tonight."

Charlie said this with some reluctance, since he was thinking about his wife. Also, he figured Harris was thinking about Katie and that Bubba's thoughts were on Kerrie. Black Jack Murdock, he figured, wasn't thinking about anybody.

Charlie continued, "Tomorrow, we'll be together from the get go."

"It might be a good idea," said Henry, "no chance for separate ambushes."

"Yeah," said Wilkie. "So it's agreed. We sleep here tonight."

"Yes, I think it's a sound strategy," said Murdock. He gave Harris what could almost pass as a fond look and added, "Of course, their strategy might be to hide and bushwhack us as a group, but one of us would remain standing, regardless. Snake River Reese would never allow that person to die in such a way."

Henry found himself being studied by all three men. "I reckon you're right," he said. "Reese has got to see who's better."

"Indeed he does," rejoined Murdock. "He is compelled to see it. He will face you and take no unfair advantage. Then, he'll be known as the man who out-gunned Henry Harris. And right now, gentlemen, nothing else matters. Not his hatred of Charlie and me, nor the wishes of his nephews, nor anything else at all."

"And how confident is he?" asked the sheriff.

Black Jack gave them a sardonic smile and said, "Oh, he is supremely confident, and that confidence won't be shaken until Henry puts a bullet right though his sanguine heart."

Wilkie pulled out his watch, glanced at it, and said, "Okay, Kate will be here shortly with our supper. Afterward, we'll patrol as before. At midnight, we'll all knock off, come back to the jail, and try to get some sleep. Anything else on your minds?" He looked up to see his three deputies staring at him.

Murdock broke the silence. "So Miss Kate is bringing our supper is she? Why you cantankerous, conniving, old buzzard. You already had this set up."

Charlie managed a chagrined look and said, "Well, set up till tomorrow, I guess. After that, it's anybody's guess."

A few minutes later, Kate and Kerrie arrived bearing containers of food.

At Sadie's Boarding House, the three Jones brothers had followed their uncle back to his room. All four men stood leaning against the walls and looking into each other's faces.

"Well," said Seth, "I reckon the fat's in the fire."

"It had to be there sooner or later," said his uncle. "Charles Wilkie is no fool. He'll try to keep himself and his deputies together. And now, it's four against four."

"What do you mean four," said James. "Wilkie only had two deputies."

"There was another one, out in the hallway."

"I didn't see him," said James. Turning to his brothers, he asked, "Did you?"

Seth shook his head, but Bud said, "I glimpsed something just behind Harris. First he was there and then he wasn't."

"Did he look familiar?" asked Reese.

"Naw," said Bud, "but it was probably Dick Wessell."

Reese walked over to the window and looked down at the street. "Doesn't matter," he said. "As long as we know how many we're up against." He turned back to his nephews.

"James, when you and Bud go back to your room, I want you to stay there. No going out."

Seth stared at his uncle and said, "I reckon this changes our plans."

Reese turned back to the window and sighed. "There are no plans anymore." There was a long silence, while the nephews watched and waited. Finally, their uncle straightened and said, "Now it's all very simple. Sometime tomorrow we meet, and as they come up we'll kill them. Just remember, Henry Harris is mine."

Wilkie watched as Kate Mulroney went around lighting more lamps, which bathed his office in an unaccustomed glow. He and his deputies sat at the table, while Kate and Kerrie filled four bowls with pungent beef stew.

Jack Murdock glanced up and said, "Would you ladies care to join us?"

"Sorry Jack," said Kate. "We have to get back to work." The two women hesitated at the door and looked back over their shoulders. Harris and Bubba stood up and followed them outside.

Alone at the table, Wilkie and Murdock smiled at each other. "Seems they have an extra reason for surviving," said Jack. "And you have a similar reason, Charlie."

"And what about Black Jack Murdock?" asked the sheriff.

"Oh, I practice survival on a twenty-four hour basis. My reasons can vary from day to day. I suppose just survival itself is sometimes incentive enough."

"Any special incentive for tomorrow?"

The black eyes burned and Murdock said, "By day's end I expect to see Snake River Reese and his mongrel kin lain out for burial. To accomplish that, we all need to survive."

Wilkie blurted the question without thinking about it. "Is Reese as good as Harris?"

"Who can say?" said Murdock. "I imagine we'll find out tomorrow."

"Yes," agreed Charlie. He paused for a moment, then said, "When you challenged Robert Reese that time, did you believe you could beat him?"

Jack Murdock lifted the napkin from beside his bowl and folded it across a bony knee. "Well Charlie, to tell you the truth, I never gave it a thought."

"Of course not," murmured Wilkie. "That's your strength."

Murdock glanced up and smiled. "Why, that's very perceptive, old friend."

"I have my moments." The door opened and the two deputies walked back in.

"That was short and sweet," called Wilkie.

"Right on both counts," said Bubba, a huge smile on his face. Harris closed the door and they both sat down. All four men continued to eat. Dawkins looked at his boss and asked, "How do you want the patrols?"

"Same as we did earlier. We'll go till midnight and then knock off."

He and Harris finished their stew. Bubba made a determined effort to eat, but Charlie could see that the young man's appetite had fled. He could also see the trepidation on Dawkins' face. Jack Murdock, of course, ate sparingly, then shoved the half-full bowl away. Finally, Charlie got up and fetched a bottle and four glasses. He poured a large shot for each of them, then stood with lifted glass. "All right, boys. What shall we drink to?"

"It's your whiskey," said Harris.

"Well then," said Charlie. "Here's to Dixie, and all her noble sons."

Black Jack Murdock rose quickly to his feet. "To Dixie," he intoned.

"To Dixie," echoed Henry and Bubba, as they got up from the table.

The men emptied their glasses and Wilkie returned the bottle to his desk. He looked over his shoulder and said, "Tomorrow, we'll finish it."

Chapter Nine

Saturday

In the pre-dawn darkness, Medford began to stir. Lamp light appeared in some of the windows and cooking smoke drifted from various chimneys. Out on the river, a stern-wheeled steamer passed abreast of the town and sounded one long, mournful note across the wide waters. This caused a flock of blackbirds to swarm from the woods and swoop out over the nearby fields. A thin, pink blush appeared on the eastern horizon, and as if on cue, a rooster crowed. He was answered by the shrill neighing of a mare. Finally, the sun rose out of a low hanging mist and hung just above the tree tops.

At Sadie's Boarding House, the proprietor and her cook bustled about in the kitchen, baking biscuits and frying eggs and bacon. A huge pot of coffee bubbled on the stove. Sadie usually ate with her boarders, but this morning she intended to stay in the kitchen. Just thinking about those wild brothers put her teeth on edge. And as for their uncle, well, he certainly had the right nickname. So like a serpent with his cold, unblinking eyes. She shivered and began carrying in food to the table.

On the floor above, Reese and the Jones brothers busied themselves with their morning preparations. Robert resolved to have a bath tonight, if circumstances permitted. He'd have a long, hot one, while recalling, in detail, the gunning of Henry Harris. He hoped for a good look at Harris's face, hoped to see the shocked look of incredulity before the eyes rolled back in his head. On the other side of the room, Seth Jones had strapped on his gun belt and was practicing a few draws. He's actually not too bad, thought Reese. Probably better than Dick Wessell. Snake River had never held a very high opinion of deputies - or sheriffs, for that matter.

In the other room, James and Bud were also putting on their clothing and strapping on the gun belts. Both pulled their pistols, spinning the cylinders and giving them a brief inspection. Like Seth, they showed a quick competence and an easy familiarity with the guns.

Reese followed his nephews down the stairs and they all walked into Sadie's dining room. Their breakfast were laid out before them. They took a seat, passed around the coffee pot, and filled their plates with bacon and eggs.

Sadie appeared in the doorway, balancing a platter of biscuits. She froze when she saw the four men, and almost dropped the dish.

Robert Reese turned and said, "Good morning, Miss Osterman."

Sadie came forward, her eyes on Reese. He presented a mocking smile and said, "I trust you slept well."

"Yes, thank you." She glanced at the brothers, took in their shoulder length hair, matted and dirty. No smiles on *those* three faces. They gazed at her as if she were a piece of meat.

Animals! The uncle was far more frightening, but at least he projected some refinement. Sadie set the platter down and hurried from the room.

Bubba Dawkins had not slept well and he was first to arise. He stepped out the back door and relieved himself, while watching the ascending sun. He buttoned up and stood there for a moment, feeling the warmth on his face. Last night's rain had cleansed the air and made it sparkle. A squirrel skittered up a pecan tree, halting once to bark a greeting over its shoulder. Above the little animal, the leaves began to stir and Bubba felt the cool touch of a breeze on his cheek. He breathed in the sweet scent of dew covered grass and wild onion. Standing there, with all his senses attuned, Bubba felt the exuberance a young man feels at simply being alive. Then the black thought came. Bubba saw it coming and tried to fend against it, but it grew and formed itself into one appalling question: *Will this be the last time? The last time I see the sun rise or smell flowers or eat breakfast?* The young man began to violently tremble. He clasped his arms and whispered, "Oh Lordy. Oh, Lordy me." After a while the trembling lessened. He turned to find Charlie Wilkie, standing behind him. The sheriff held a double-barreled shotgun in his hand.

Dawkins let his arms drop and murmured, "Good morning."

The sheriff looked closely at his deputy. "How're you doing, Bubba?"

Bubba lowered his head and said, "Not too good, Charlie."

"Goddammit, you look at me when you speak!"

The sheriff's shout hit him like an open palm across his face.

Bubba jumped and took a step backward. His eyes bugged out and he stared in shocked astonishment at his boss. Wilkie stood red-faced and rigid, the chin jutting forward. His eyes bored into Bubba's. "Are you my Chief Deputy or not?"

Dawkins finally found his voice and answered, "Why yeah, Charlie."

"Well, start acting like it then. And stop thinking of yourself. You've got a job to do."

Bubba straightened and his face flushed. He looked Wilkie in the eye and said, "All right, maybe I was thinking about myself. And maybe I'm scared, but when the time comes, I'll do my job. Now if you don't believe that, you can just go to hell."

Charlie regarded the young man for a long moment and his face softened. He held the shotgun up and said, "I never see one of these without thinking about a young bartender in the Butterfly Saloon. With this in his hand, that man made *other* people afraid."

Bubba felt his tension start to leave. In a lowered voice, he said, "Like dress shop bandits and such."

The sheriff extended the gun toward his deputy. "I want you to carry this today."

"Why me?"

"Because you ain't as good with a six shooter as me. That's nothing to fret about. I ain't as good as Murdock, and Murdock sure ain't as good as Harris. If you weren't around, I'd be carrying this thing."

Bubba nodded and took the shotgun.

"Give 'em one barrel at a time," said Charlie. "Then you can use that cannon you carry."

"I'll be there when the time comes," said Bubba.

"I know you will, deputy. I knew it when I hired you." Wilkie turned and went back through the door. He left it slightly ajar and Bubba could hear him talking to Harris and Murdock. "I gave Dawkins the shotgun. Figured we could use the extra firepower."

"Uh-huh," came Henry's slow voice. "I know what you were thinking. Give Bubba the shotgun and maybe he'll save your ass again."

Charlie laughed and Bubba found himself laughing along with him. He cracked open the gun and saw the two shells, nestled in each chamber. He snapped the shotgun shut and headed for the doorway. For some reason, he felt a whole lot better.

Katie looked up to see the four men coming through the door. Her eyes lingered on Harris, who walked in first, followed by the others. His eyes flicked to the barroom doors, then to the dining room. He turned toward Katie and they gazed at each other for a moment. She instinctively understood. He was their point man. Wherever they go today, he'll be in the lead. They don't want to get in the way of his gun. Last night, Reese and the Jones brothers had sent a chill down her spine, but the sight of these four gave her instant comfort. Here come my big brothers, she thought. Now let me see you try something. Even Bubba Dawkins qualified, though he was much younger than she. They came abreast of Kate and Harris gave her a wink.

"Want to have breakfast with us?" he asked.

"Sure, but I can't until Kerrie gets here. She's running late this morning."

Bubba turned a troubled face to Wilkie and said, "I'm gonna go see about her."

Wilkie saw the determined look in his eyes and felt he had to humor him. He paused, for a moment, then said, "Okay, but take that scatter gun with you. And if you catch sight of that bunch, you high-tail it right back over here."

The deputy nodded and walked quickly through the door, the huge Colt Dragoon jouncing against his side.

Kate said, "You fellows go ahead and take a table. I'll be over as soon as Kerrie and her guardian get back."

They started past and she touched Henry on the arm. He halted and she whispered, "You won't go and get yourself killed, will you?"

He grinned and said, "I'll try not to."

Kate walked back to her desk and the three men found a table by the window. They were just in time to see Dawkins disappear around the corner.

Wilkie craned his neck toward the glass and said, "I don't see a living soul."

"I imagine the good citizens have secured themselves inside," said Murdock. "The whole town knows what's coming."

"I shouldn't have let Bubba leave."

"He was determined to go," said Jack, "and he wanted to go alone. I don't think you could have stopped him. Anyway, he'll do exactly what you told him."

Marge Blackwell came over to take their orders. Charlie looked up to tell her they were going to hold off till Katie arrived. Jack and Henry were staring out at the street, waiting for Bubba to come back round the corner. Charlie began to speak, but nobody heard the words. All anybody heard was the shattering *BRROOOM* that shook the restaurant window and echoed down the street. The men knew that sound could only come from a twelve gauge shotgun. It was immediately followed by the sharp crack of a pistol. The men leapt to their feet, upending the table and sending silverware clattering across the room. Marge jumped aside as they rushed past her and out the door. They were halfway down the street when the shotgun roared again.

* * *

Bubba walked down the center of the street so he'd have a good view of the buildings. Glancing around, he was surprised to find the street deserted. Then the reason occurred to him and he felt empty inside. All the citizens were hiding. He gave the windows a closer look. Behind a few of them, people stared out with wide and anxious eyes. He turned right and headed down Locust Street. Kerrie's house stood on the left, about mid-way down. Bubba quickened his pace. He reached the house, just as she walked out on the front porch.

"Bubba? Is that you?" she asked, lifting a hand to shade her eyes from the sun.

Why did he always grin like a fool when he saw Kerrie? He was doing it again. "Yep, it's me."

"You told me all of you were sticking together today."

"We are, but Charlie let me split off to come and get you."

"Not a good idea, Bubba. I don't need an escort and you shouldn't be out by yourself." Bubba's face fell and Kerrie touched him on the arm. "But I'm glad you came," she added

The stable boy sat slack-jawed on the floor, rubbing his temple where the man's open palm had landed.

Bud Jones glanced over his shoulder as he fitted a bridle to one of the horses. "I told 'em," he said to the boy. "I never seen a livery stable yet could take proper care of a horse."

"I *was* taking care of them," said the boy.

"The hell you was," shouted Jones. "If you was taking care of them, how did this one get a limp?"

"He was limping when the other man rode him in."

Bud regarded the stable boy with narrowed eyes. "That 'other man' you're talking about happens to be Snake River Reese, and if he sees his horse in this condition, he's gonna shoot you right between the eyes."

The boy got to his feet and said, "Don't tell him it was my fault, Mister. I tried to take care of him. Caint you smell the liniment on his leg?"

Bud had already smelled it. He led the buckskin out of the stall and stood looking down at the stable boy. "Well, you just make sure I don't find anything wrong with the other three. I'm gonna walk this one down the street and see how bad the limp is. Did you feed them this morning?"

"Yes sir. I fed 'em about half an hour ago."

"Did you brush 'em down last night?"

"You can see I did," said the boy, still rubbing the side of his head.

Bud lifted a finger. "Don't get smart."

He led his uncle's horse through the stable door and began walking him up the street. All the time, he kept looking back and watching the left foreleg. *Damn stable boys. They just don't care about horses.* Actually, Bud had met few men anywhere who cared about them as much as he did.

Uncle Robert hadn't wanted him to go out this morning. Bud had to practically beg him. Hell, they couldn't stay together every minute. Now, his uncle would be glad he'd let him check on their horses. Bud came to the intersection of Locust and Main. He saw the sheriff's office straight ahead, down near the end of the street. Better not get any closer than this, he thought. He tugged on the horse's rein and turned to the left. Jones walked slowly, looking back and observing the horse's gait. The limp was getting better. He'd probably walk it out. He was still intent on the horse when he heard a woman's gasp. Bud whirled to the front and saw the sheriff's deputy. He was pushing the woman away and at the same time raising a sawed-off shotgun. Jones dropped the horse's reins and reached for his pistol.

The couple had started up the street, both squinting into the mounting sun. As they neared the junction with main street, a man turned the corner and walked toward them. He was leading a horse and looking back at the horse's forelegs. To Dawkins, man and horse were just a shadowy, shifting mass against the streaming sunlight. The wavering form drew closer and came into focus and there was Bud Jones, still looking back at the horse.

Kerrie gasped, and without thinking, Dawkins pushed her aside. Bud's head snapped around and he saw the deputy standing there with the partially raised shotgun. For a long moment, neither man moved. Then Bud Jones went for his weapon.

"Nooo!" screamed Kerrie, as Bubba brought up the shotgun.

The sun shone in Bubba's eyes, but the man's movement had been unmistakable. An explosion sounded in his ears and Bubba was surprised to realize he'd already fired the shot gun. He also realized he had missed. The buckshot whistled past the man, grazing the horse's neck. The horse reared and whirled away, ripping the reins from Bud's hand. He leaped forward, bringing his pistol up and centering the barrel on the deputy's chest. Jones squeezed the trigger and Bubba spun around and fell face forward in a mud puddle. Bud approached the motionless figure. He rolled the body over with his foot and saw where his slug had pierced the chest. The lawman's shirt was drenched and sticking to the skin. The woman screamed and Jones looked toward her. Then he looked back down again and this time he was gazing into the twin bores of a twelve gauge. They looked like two dark tunnels. The deputy's white face shone above them. Then, as Bud watched, the tunnels seemed to grow larger and darker until they filled up all the space in front of him and finally filled up all his world. Jones never heard the shotgun blast or felt the buckshot, ripping into his skull. He pitched backward onto the street and lay motionless in the mud.

Bubba lay very still and felt a numbness spreading across his chest. He didn't know if he'd killed the man or not, but was betting that he had. This time, he'd taken proper aim, and just before he pulled that trigger the second time, he'd seen the look of abject terror on Bud Jones's face. Kerrie was pressing her hand against his wound and he could hear her racking sobs. He tried to put his arm around her, but he could not lift it from the ground.

The deputy closed his eyes while the deadness expanded across his shoulders and down into his stomach. I didn't really need to be so afraid, he thought. Facing him wasn't so bad. Even dying isn't so bad. You do what you have to do. He thought about Wilkie and the others. They'll finish it, he thought. They'll take care of Reese and the rest of his bastard nephews. Bubba sank down into darkness and gave a shudder of dread. Then, his lips moved in a smile as he recalled the image of Henry Harris, standing cool and competent. And that image, for the second time, relieved him of his fear.

"Damn, what was that?" cried James when he heard the roar of the shotgun. A few seconds later came the sharp crack of a revolver.

Seth Jones turned to Reese and yelled, "I told you not to

let him go. The damn horses could have waited."

All three men were on their feet and pushing past the dining table. The two brothers charged out the door first, with their uncle trotting behind them. They reached the street and slid to a stop. The second shotgun blast had just swept over them in a shattering burst of sound.

Henry, Charlie, and Jack came pounding up the street with mud flying from their boots. They were nearing Locust Street when they saw three men trotting south to meet them. They came to a halt and waited.

"Fan out," said Charlie. His voice was crisp and cool. He walked to the left, while Murdock edged over to the right. Harris remained in the center of the street. Reese and the Jones brothers slowed to a walk and they, in turn, began to spread out. Then they came forward in a line and stopped just short of the intersection. Harris and Reese's eyes were fixed on each other.

Finally, James's voice broke the silence. "Oh Christ, Seth. Look over yonder."

Seth Jones peered around his uncle and looked down Locust Street. A horse was rearing wildly, blood streaming down it's neck. Near the horse, a man lay crumpled in the mire, and just beyond the horse and man, was a bundle of bright clothing. It took a moment for him to realize it was a kneeling woman, wearing a blue dress. She swayed to one side and Seth saw that she was huddled over a second man. He perceived a flash of light. It was the sun, glinting off Bubba's bronze star.

"Robert," he said. "Bud and the deputy are down."

Harris and Reese had not taken their eyes off each other

and it was Harris who spoke first. "Your nephews want to care for their brother and we want to tend to our friend. After that, they can stand aside and you and I will settle it."

Reese nodded, and for the first time, looked away from Harris. He glanced to the left and his body froze. Black Jack Murdock was staring back at him.

"Of course, sir," stated the dark man, "if you feel this situation needs an immediate resolution, I would suggest you pull that pistol and get to work. Time and place are of complete indifference to me."

The gunfighter's ashy eyes widened and he regarded Jack for a moment. For once, he seemed slightly disconcerted. "So you've joined up with Wilkie again."

"'Joined up' is a slightly inaccurate phrase. Charles Wilkie is my friend. I am here to assist him in his time of need."

"Where's Wessell?" asked the gunman.

"Unknown," said Murdock. "He could be anywhere."

"Not likely. Wessell's gone and you're here to take up some slack."

"I am at your service, sir."

"For God's sake, Robert. Let's go see about Bud." Even as he spoke, James was hurrying toward the still figures on Locust Street.

Reese nodded at Seth and said, "Okay, we'll all go together."

Wilkie went first, followed closely by the other four. The horse galloped past him, blood flying from its neck, and he halted for a moment, taking in the carnage. James was kneeling beside his brother and puking in the mud. Beyond, lay Bubba, his head cradled in Kerrie's lap. Jones looked up, wiped the vomit from his lips, and stared at the sheriff. As Charlie hurried passed, James drew his revolver, and still kneeling, shot him in the side.

The heavy caliber bullet passed between Wilkie's ribs

and ranged upward, smashing into his heart. The sheriff gave a startled grunt and plunged forward into the blood-mixed muck. His face came to rest a few inches from Kerrie's knee, and he stared and her and Bubba with vacant, lifeless eyes.

His killer glanced wildly about, and then his eyes locked on one gaunt figure and remained there. Murdock was standing slightly sideways and perfectly still, his long right arm extended and his pistol centered on the kneeling man. James tried once to lift his weapon, but his arm had turned to lead. He opened his mouth to speak, but whether in supplication or defiance, nobody ever knew. Murdock thumbed the hammer on his pistol and shot Jones in the face.

Harris could give no attention to what was going on around him. He must once again focus on Snake River Reese. Not to do so would mean his death and probably John Murdock's. The moment was here. He was about to make the instant connect between thought and action when he heard another shot.

Jack Murdock staggered forward. He regained his balance and turned round to face his assailant, the thin legs shifting to keep him erect. The slug had passed straight through his body, leaving a spreading stain in back and front. He saw Seth standing with a smoking pistol in his fist. Jones screamed an oath and fired again. This time the bullet ripped through Murdock's left side.

The dark man wavered and felt life draining out of him, felt a coldness sweep across his body. The light around him brightened, then darkened, and a humming sound rose in his ears. A feeling of looseness came over him as his thin knees bent and he sank toward the ground.

Seth gave a yell and lifted his gun for one more shot. Then, in the moment of his triumph, he beheld the final madness and the ultimate splendor of Black Jack Murdock.

The gaunt figure before him had refused to collapse. The

knees locked themselves in place, then slowly straightened. Murdock rose to his full height, took a few halting steps toward his attacker, and raised his own weapon. Seth seemed mesmerized by what he was watching, much as his brother had been. Jack fired and the bullet caught Jones just below the Adam's apple. The blood gushed forth and flowed down over his collar. Seth dropped his weapon, clutched his throat, and tumbled onto his back. Murdock moved stiff-legged toward him. He stood over the fallen man and watched him in his agony. And in a clear voice he said, "I'm afraid, sir, that our interview is concluded."

Then, taking careful aim, he fired down at the gasping brother. The bullet entered precisely between the eyes. Murdock swayed once, then sprawled across the body of his victim. He took one shuddering breath and the black eyes closed forever.

From the corner of his eye, Harris had seen it all, and for the first time in his life, he felt shock and horror and a sense of irreparable loss. He tried to fight through it and focus on his opponent. On Robert Reese's face, he saw no emotion at all, because Snake River had cleared his mind of everything except the matter at hand. In a moment, he would watch Harris fall.

Henry waited for the familiar iciness to lay onto his being, that feeling of detachment which would nerve his body and clear his brain. He waited but that feeling did not come. And then he knew it never would. This butchery which had cost him his companions, left him with only a numbing remorse and a sense of utter despair. Facing Robert Reese, he took a step backward, then another, and another, while this morning's slaughter lay before him, like some hideous counterpoint to the sparkling air and brilliant sunshine.

All dead. All dead, he thought, and only the two

gunfighters, the least worthy of the lot, left standing. He looked into the washed out eyes of Snake River Reese, and as he watched, those eyes grew slightly wider. Reese's hand blurred toward his gun.

Kerrie could not leave Bubba Dawkins lying in the mud, and so the young woman, now shocked into a trance-like stupor, must witness one more killing and add another image to her store of nightmares.

And here to accommodate her was Henry Harris and Snake River Reese. The two men stood about fifteen feet apart, facing one another. They looked like a couple of townsman who'd paused on the street to pass the time of day. Recalling it later, she figured she must have blinked, because now she saw the men in a slightly different pose. One was holding a pistol down by his right side and the other had just fired his gun into that man's stomach. She had detected no movement between the first image she'd seen and the second. Wide-eyed, she watched Robert Reese stagger backward and attempt to raise his weapon. Harris fired once more. Reese shuddered as the bullet struck him. Then his knees buckled and he crumpled to the ground. Kerrie Doster would always remember the expression on the falling man's face. It was almost comical, that look of disbelief.

Coda

The following Monday, Harris checked out of his room and walked to the Medford City Bank. Delbert Wilson, the bank president, ushered him into his office and offered him a seat. The portly executive knelt before a floor safe and extracted a white envelope. He rose with a grunt, opened the envelope, and laid ten one hundred dollar bills on the desk.

Henry stared at them for a moment, then picked up the money and said, "Give me that envelope, Delbert." He replaced the bills in the envelope and returned it to the banker. "I understand the town's taking up a collection for the sheriff's widow. Add this money to it."

Delbert said, "Are you sure you want to do this, Henry? God knows you've earned your bonus."

"Yes, I'm sure."

"Well, I'll give this to Mrs. Wilkie separately, *and* I'll tell her where it came from."

"No, don't do that," said Harris. "Just say it's from a grateful town." He rose and shook hands with Wilson.

"Henry, I just want you to know that I... Well hell, the whole town owes—"

"It's all right, Delbert."

"I guess you'll be getting back to that farm now."

"Yep, I'll start back sometime today. Got a couple of stops to make first."

He walked south on Main Street and felt the sun baking into his shoulders. A hot wind swept up the street, bringing a swirling dust devil. He turned in at Sadie's Boarding House, climbed the stairs, and knocked on one of the doors. A young woman, pale but pretty, opened it and gave him a smile. From the bed behind her, came a voice:

"Is that you, Henry?"

Bubba Dawkins lay propped against two huge pillows, a broad bandage wound about his chest, only slightly whiter than the face above it.

Harris smiled and asked, "How's it going, deputy?"

"Not too bad." Glancing at Kerrie, he added, "I got a good nurse."

"Well, your nurse has to go to work," she said. Leaning over, she kissed Bubba on the cheek and nodded to Harris. Before closing the door behind her, she turned and said, "I'll stop by on my way home."

Harris walked over and stood at the foot of the bed. "What does the doctor say?"

"Oh, he says I'll live if infection don't set in. Says I was real lucky. The bullet went straight through. It nicked a rib, but missed the lung and spine."

"Well, you're a young man, Bubba. You'll heal up fast. What do you figure you'll do when you're back on your feet?"

Dawkins closed his eyes and sighed. "They tell me I'm still drawing a deputy's pay."

"You sure are."

"Well, I reckon I'll just keep on doing that." He looked up at Harris with haunted eyes. "Do you think that's what Charlie would have wanted?"

"I'm sure of it," said Harris. "As a matter of fact, some of the townies are talking about appointing you temporary sheriff. I think Charlie would approve of that, too."

"Yeah, I heard that rumor, but I don't know if I can . . . "

"Sure you can, Bubba. At least until the next election. Then, if you decide you don't want it, don't run."

The two men were silent for a moment. Finally, Bubba said, "Dosh Colson's gonna serve as deputy until I'm up and about. Maybe I can get him to keep the job under me."

"Don't count on it," said Henry. "He'll want to get back to his saloon and Katie will make sure he does."

"I guess you're right."

"Anyway, there's plenty of prospects around. Just find one that'll listen to what you tell him."

Suddenly, the young man strained upward and said, "He saved my life, Henry. Charlie saved my life when he gave me that shotgun. The sun was in my eyes. I was hit and I just . . ."

"I know, but you did real good, Bubba. Real good."

"I saw everything that happened, Henry."

Harris gave him a surprised look. "You saw it all?"

"I watched Charlie and Jack die, and then I watched you." He gazed at Harris and in a subdued voice said, "Snake River Reese was a famous gunfighter and he never had a chance. He wasn't even close."

"The sun was in *his* eyes, too," said Harris

"Didn't matter. He was a dead man either way."

Henry walked over to the window and looked down on one of the side streets. A long-eared hound was lying in the shade of an elm tree. It sensed it was being observed and looked up at Harris with sad, soulful eyes.

"You know," said Bubba, "all our planning didn't amount to a hill of beans, did it? When the time came, things just sort of went forward on their on."

"That's the way it usually happens," said Harris.

"And who would have thought Charlie would be blindsided the way he was, the best lawmen of us all."

Henry did not mention to Bubba that, at the time, the sheriff was focused on helping his deputy. He stared at the hound and said, "They're burying the Jones brothers today, out at their old home place. Took 'em over this morning. Their uncle will be going in the ground beside them."

He looked at the man on the bed. "Jack and Charlie were buried yesterday, out at the Medford Cemetery."

"I heard," said Bubba. "I wish I could have gone."

"Yeah, the whole town turned out. There were even some musicians there. I don't think I've ever seen musicians at a funeral before."

"Really? What kind of music did they play?"

"It was kind of standard for Charlie. They played at his grave first. I believe it was *Amazing Grace.*"

"What did they play for Jack Murdock?"

"I think they intended to do the same song, but I asked for a different one."

"What was it, Henry?"

Harris turned back to the window. "*The Bonnie Blue Flag.* It's an old confederate tune."

He glanced over his shoulder, then looked back out the glass. Looking at the hound was better than watching Bubba's tears. "They were good men," he added.

"They were good friends," said the deputy.

Harris walked over and stood, for a moment, looking down at Bubba. He slowly unbuckled his gun belt and laid it across the bed.

"Henry. No. I caint take that. Why I wouldn't . . . "

"Take it," said Harris. "Sooner or later, you may have need of it. I doubt that I ever will."

Bubba Dawkins raised his head and gazed at the gift. Then he lay back and covered his face with his hands. Harris patted the deputy on the shoulder, walked out of the room, and closed the door behind him.

He strode over to the livery stable and waited while the stable boy saddled the gray. "What's it come to?" he asked, reaching for his billfold.

"Nothing," said the boy. "Sheriff Wilkie said the county would take care of it. I reckon they will."

Harris flipped him a silver dollar and mounted the mare. He noticed the boy, still watching him in his simple-minded way. "Something else?"

"Your friend, Mr. Murdock. He was real polite, but he kinda scared me."

"He scared a lot of people."

"But he was a real gentleman," added the boy. "I liked him."

"Well," said Harris. "You're not alone there." He reined the horse around and trotted down the street.

As he approached the hotel, Kate Mulroney stepped out the front door and stood there waiting for him. Henry reined up and sat looking down at her. Kate's brown eyes strayed to his waist.

"Where's the pistol?" she asked.

"I left it with Bubba. He may find a use for it."

"And you won't?"

"There's a rifle and a shotgun at the farm. That's all you need for game."

Kate nodded and said, "I wonder if Henry Harris has taken another turn in the road."

"It's possible," he said. Reaching down, he touched her hair and added, "You look beautiful, Katie"

She seized his hand, kissed it, and took a step backward. "When will I see you again?"

"Soon as I can get away."

"Maybe I'll ride up and visit you first. I haven't seen the place in awhile."

"Katherine Mulroney," he grinned. "I think that's a fine idea."

Harris wheeled about and headed back up Main Street. He noticed people pausing to watch him pass. A few gave him a friendly wave. The horseman nodded to either side and kept going. He passed out of town and rode northward, traveling though a vast expanse of fertile fields. Toward sundown, he approached the rising hills of Crowley's Ridge. Harris paused for a moment, debating whether to pitch camp or keep riding in the dark. He decided to go on. After all, he knew the way well enough, and he needed to see his farm.

~The End~

About the Author

H. R. Williams grew up on Crowley's Ridge, a line of hills and a geographical region that figures in many of his stories. The author refers to this area as "my own Yoknapatawpha County." He was a paratrooper in the 101st Airborne Division and held about a thousand jobs (slight exaggeration) before coming to the conclusion that his only talent lay in writing. Since then, his short fiction and essays have appeared in a wide assortment of national and regional magazines. His mystery novel, *The Whiskey Killing,* represented by the August Agency in New York City, was recently purchased by Five Star Publications. Mr. Williams is husband to Nora Lee (long suffering and ever patient) and the father of four children.